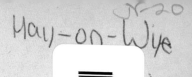

SPY-CATCHE

'What if I were to tell you al
I've seen acting in a very su
way?' said Holly. 'A specific
seems to spend an awful lot of time
scribbling stuff down in a little booklet.'

'Who?' asked Miranda. 'What sort
of stuff?'

'I don't know,' said Holly. 'That's the
whole point. He would be the perfect
target for our first investigation.'

'You're sure this won't get us into any
trouble?' Miranda said.

'There's always an element of risk if
you're going to be a spy,' Holly said. 'But
if we're clever, he won't even know he's
being watched.'

'OK,' said Miranda. 'I'm with you. Tell
me about it.'

'Meet me at the front gates after school,
and I'll take you to where I've seen him,'
Holly whispered. 'And remember,' she
said. 'Not a word to anyone!'

The Mystery Kids series

1 Spy-Catchers!
2 Lost and Found

THE MYSTERY KiDS
Spy-Catchers!

Fiona Kelly

Hodder
Children's
Books

a division of Hodder Headline plc

Special thanks to Allan Frewin Jones

Copyright © 1995 Ben M. Baglio
Created by Ben M. Baglio
London W6 0HE
First published in Great Britain in 1995
by Hodder Children's Books

A Catalogue record for this book is
available from the British Library

ISBN 0 340 61989 9

Typeset by Hewer Text Composition Services, Edinburgh
Printed and bound in Great Britain by
Cox & Wyman Ltd, Reading, Berks.

Hodder Children's Books
A Division of Hodder Headline plc
338 Euston Road
London
NW1 3BH

Contents

To Tristan, Lauren, Alison, Tanzen, Henry, George, Jocelyn, Amanda and Rachel

Spy-Catchers Ltd

Holly Adams held her breath, her grey eyes widening, her mouth half-open as she watched the shadowy figure glide silently around the darkened street corner.

Look behind you! Look behind you! she wanted to scream as a glint of grey metal in the man's hand caught the light. He had a gun!

But it wasn't the man with the gun that she was desperate to warn. It was another man, who was walking along the rain-swept street, wrapped in a long grey coat, unaware of the peril that was creeping up on him. A handsome man with a rugged, dependable face and a curl of black hair at his forehead. Secret Agent John Raven. Holly's hero.

Every hair on her head stood to attention as the gunman lifted his weapon and aimed it at the other's back.

1

Crack! The sharp echo of the gun made Holly jump almost out of her skin.

Her spoon fell out of her hand, spilling milky cornflakes all over the couch.

'For heaven's sake, Holly! Watch what you're doing!' her mother complained from the other end of the couch.

A blaze of music swelled from the television as the credits rolled.

'He shot him! He shot him!' yelled Holly, almost tipping the cereal bowl out of her lap.

'I doubt it,' said Mrs Adams. 'He's got to be in next week's episode.' She aimed the remote control at the television and the screen went blank. 'And now, my girl, I think it's time you were in bed, don't you?'

'I wish they wouldn't *do* that,' said Holly. 'Now I've got to wait until next week to find out if he's going to be all right.'

'Trust me,' said her mother. 'He'll be all right. Finish your cornflakes.' She stood up, and looked down at Holly. 'I'm not at all sure you should be watching this sort of thing at your age,' she said. 'Not with *your* imagination.'

Holly looked up, pushing her long brown

2

hair behind her ears and grinning. 'I'm *twelve*,' she said, putting the bowl down on the carpet. 'I'm not a *kid*. I do know it's not real. I can't help it if I get involved in it, can I?' She unfolded her long thin legs and stood up. 'How do you think he's going to get out of it?' she asked her mother.

'I expect he'll spin round and catch the bullet in his teeth,' said Mrs Adams. 'I'm sure secret agents are taught tricks like that.'

Holly frowned at her. 'That's silly,' she said. 'He's more likely to be wearing a bullet-proof vest.' Her eyebrows knitted as she thought. 'Or the entire coat might be made of some bullet-proof material. Or . . . or . . . he'll have heard something.' She paced experimentally across the carpet, listening for the sound of her own footfalls.

'Some small sound,' she said, disappointed that her socked feet made no sound on the carpet. 'The sort of thing that ordinary people wouldn't even hear. The sort of thing only a trained spy-catcher would notice. The single squeak of a shoe.' She ducked into an alert crouch. 'And then he'll go – *whoosh*! – into a doorway.' She jumped sideways. 'Oops!' Her foot landed in the cereal bowl she'd left

3

on the floor, sending a splosh of soggy cornflakes up her leg and over the carpet.

'Holly!' howled Mrs Adams. 'Be *careful*!'

Holly stood on one leg, dangling her wet foot in the air. 'Sorry,' she said. 'I slipped. I'll get a cloth.'

'I'm going to stop you watching these spy serials,' said Mrs Adams. 'I'm not sure what it's doing to your *mind*, but I know it's ruining my carpet!'

Holly ran through into the kitchen and came back with a cloth. 'Can I phone Miranda?' she asked from her hands and knees as she scooped up the mush and dropped it back into the bowl. Miranda Hunt was Holly's best friend.

'No, you can't,' said Mrs Adams. 'At this time of night? She'll be in bed.'

'No, she won't,' said Holly. 'She watches *Spyglass*, too.' She gave her mother a pleading look. 'I only want a very quick word with her. Just to see how she thinks John Raven gets out of being shot.'

'It can wait until the morning,' Mrs Adams said very determinedly. 'You can discuss it with her then. Now, if you've finishing mopping up, you can take that bowl through into

4

the kitchen, and then you can go to bed and *dream* about spies as much as you like.'

'I hope I do,' said Holly. 'I've decided I'm going to be a spy when I leave school.'

Her mother smiled. 'I'm glad to hear you're prepared to wait that long,' she said. 'You're not usually so patient.'

Holly gave her mother a goodnight kiss before running into the kitchen.

'Will Dad come in and say goodnight when he gets home?' Holly called as she tipped the remains of her evening snack into the bin.

'I expect so,' said Mrs Adams. 'If he's not too late. Now stop *shouting*, Holly. You'll wake Jamie up.'

'Huh!' said Holly. 'You could explode a bomb on his pillow and it wouldn't wake him up.' Jamie was Holly's younger brother. Nine years old, and an absolute menace.

Mrs Adams came out into the hall. 'Bed!' she said. 'Sweet dreams.'

Holly was halfway up the stairs. She turned round, a big grin on her face. 'I don't want *sweet* dreams,' she said. 'I'm going to dream about catching foreign spies!'

Ten minutes later she was in bed, all ready to read a couple of chapters of her new

5

mystery book before she went to sleep. Holly loved mystery books. Her shelves were full of them. But even her packed shelves weren't as full of mysteries as her imagination.

Holly lived in Highgate, in North London. Now, London, she often thought to herself, must be simply *teeming* with foreign spies. Spying on the Royal Family, and spying on the Houses of Parliament and on all those government buildings down by the River Thames. Sinister men in long dark coats with the collars pulled up. Sneaking through the streets at the dead of night with pistols bulging in their armpits and cameras no bigger than ballpoint pens sewn into their lapels.

Her bedroom door opened and her mother's face appeared. 'No reading tonight,' said Mrs Adams. 'It's late, and you've got school in the morning.' She smiled. 'Come on, Holly, put that book away and turn off the light. Even spies need their sleep.'

'OK,' sighed Holly.

It was all very well her mother telling her to go to sleep, but as Holly lay in the darkness she felt totally wide awake. She lay there with her eyes open, listening to the noises from the street.

6

Clack, clack, clack, clack. A woman walking past in high-heeled shoes. The distant yowl of a cat. The muffled roar of passing cars. The faint purr of an aeroplane, taking people to foreign countries to do exciting things.

A car drew up outside. She heard the engine stop suddenly and the thud of the door being closed. She scrambled on to her knees and down to the foot of the bed to draw a corner of her curtain aside. It was her father, home from another late night at the office.

Mr Adams always seemed to be working late these days, even though Holly *knew* he didn't like his job. His real love was to be down in the cellar with his woodworking tools, making things for their home.

When she had asked him about his long hours at the office, he had told her they needed the money.

'I don't mind having less pocket money, if it means you can come home earlier,' she had told him.

He had given her a big hug. 'Don't you worry about it,' he'd said. 'One day I'll give up that rotten job and be a full-time furniture-maker. You'll see. One day.'

She saw her father walk round the car

and head for the house. But something else caught her attention. There was a strange shape over on the far side of the street. Leaning up against a wall, shrouded in shadows.

A man? A strange man lurking, perfectly still and quiet in the dark, between the streetlights. Holly rubbed her eyes. Was it a man? Why would anyone be standing there at this time of night? Unless they were keeping watch.

Holly lowered herself until only her eyes showed over the window. It couldn't be a *spy*, surely? Not around here. What was there to spy on? But it could be a burglar. Waiting for the house lights to go off before creeping across to do his wicked deeds while everyone was asleep.

Holly's heart pounded. The man hadn't made a move. Talk about suspicious!

Her heart bounced up into her throat as she heard her bedroom door open.

'Holly? What on earth are you up to?' asked her father, coming into the room, his coat still on.

She looked round at him. 'Quick! There's someone watching the house,' she breathed. 'I think it's a burglar!'

8

'A *burglar*?' said Mr Adams, his eyebrows lifting as he walked across to the window. 'Where?'

'There!' Holly whispered, stabbing her finger at the window. 'Keep down or he'll see you.'

Mr Adams pulled the curtain open and looked out.

'Hoy!' he shouted. 'You! Mr Burglar! Hop it, or we'll call the police.' He looked at Holly. 'I think,' he said with a grin, 'that you'll find your burglar is a roll of old carpet someone has left out for the dustmen!'

Holly pressed her nose up against the window.

'Oh!' Disappointment and relief made her feel all shivery inside. 'Well, it *looked* like a burglar,' she said.

'Come on,' said her father. 'Back to bed, before your mum comes up and catches you.'

Holly pulled the bedclothes over herself. 'It might have been a burglar,' she said. 'It's best to be on the safe side. I'm just reading in my new book about this burglar called the Cat. He can climb right up sheer walls and get in through upstairs windows

9

without making a sound. The last house he was in—'

'Tell me about it tomorrow,' interrupted her father. 'You don't want to go frightening yourself by thinking about burglars all night.'

'Burglars don't frighten me,' Holly said, rather insulted. 'I could soon deal with a burglar.' She sat up. 'All you'd need would be a big net, spread out on the floor and attached to a trip wire. One wrong step and *zip*! He'd be head over heels up in the air. All neatly packaged for the police.'

Mr Adams laughed. 'I can see I'm going to have to watch where I'm walking from now on,' he said. 'We'd better put a notice on the front door: "Beware of the Holly".'

'It's a good trap, though, isn't it?' said Holly. 'And I've thought of some others.'

'Just so long as you don't booby-trap the house without warning us,' said her father. 'But right this minute, I think you should be getting off to sleep.'

Her father closed the door and her room became dark again.

Holly lay wide-eyed in the darkness, making plans for her spy-catching career.

10

Spy-catchers! Holly and Miranda, Spy-Catchers Ltd. No, that didn't sound professional enough. Adams and Hunt. That would be better. Adams and Hunt, Spy-Catchers Ltd. They'd have an office with their names on the door in gold lettering. Two desks. A filing cabinet filled with important information.

Holly yawned and snuggled under the covers.

I haven't got time for sleep, she thought drowsily. She had to think about all the stuff they'd need. Invisible-ink pens. Secret cameras. Brief-cases with hidden pockets. Communication devices made to look like wristwatches.

Miranda and I will have to write all this down tomorrow, she thought. *We'll need a notebook for a start*.

A few moments later she was fast asleep.

Holly's big idea

At breakfast the next morning, Holly was still trying to work out how Secret Agent John Raven might have escaped his enemy's bullet.

'Rocket boots,' said Jamie, after she had explained Secret Agent Raven's predicament.

'What do you mean, *rocket boots*?' asked Holly.

'Miniature rockets in the heels of his boots,' Jamie explained between mouthfuls of cereal. 'He could use a device in his pocket to make them work. Like ejector seats in aeroplanes. He just presses a button and – *zoom!* – ten metres, straight up in the air!'

'That's ridiculous,' said Holly. 'He'd break his neck when he landed.'

'He could have a parachute hidden down the back of his coat,' Jamie insisted, not keen to let go of his idea without a fight. He looked

12

across the table at his mother. 'Why can't I stay up to see *Spyglass*?' he asked.

'Because you're too young and it's on too late,' his mother replied from behind her newspaper.

'Dad?' asked Jamie. 'I'm not too young, am I?'

His father looked up from some documents he was reading.

'Yes,' he said. 'If your mother says you're too young, then you're too young.' He gave his family a bemused look. 'Too young for what?'

'Don't worry about it,' said Mrs Adams. 'It's time you two were setting off for school.'

'But you let Holly watch it,' Jamie complained.

Holly got up from the table, sticking her tongue out at Jamie.

'Mum! Holly poked her tongue out at me!' said Jamie.

'Holly, don't poke your tongue out at your brother. It's not nice,' said Mrs Adams without looking up from her newspaper.

On her way to school, Holly kept her eyes peeled for suspicious-looking people.

An old woman hobbled slowly along the

pavement on the other side of the road. But *was* it an old woman? It could easily be some heavily disguised foreign agent. And what about that woman with the push-chair? Was that *really* a baby in there? Or was it a doll with a secret panel in its tummy, crammed full of stolen documents?

The toddler threw a toy out of the push-chair.

OK, so this time it was *a real baby*, thought Holly. *But that's just the sort of thing secret agents* would *do*.

She turned the corner into the road leading to her school. It was a modern building, all glass and concrete and white-painted metal, set in wide grassy grounds, with red gravel playing-areas over to one side. *The Thomas Petheridge Comprehensive*, the sign announced.

The pavement outside and the area in front of the school were dotted with pupils, some of them standing in clumps and chatting, and others making their way towards the entrance.

'Holly!' Miranda's yell sounded above the general level of noise like the call of a bugle. Miranda had one of the loudest voices Holly

14

had ever heard. It went into overdrive when she laughed. Holly was convinced you could hear Miranda Hunt's laugh five kilometres away, if the wind was in the right direction.

Miranda came bounding towards her, her long corn-blonde hair flying out behind her like a banner, her round face beaming with excitement. She was shorter than Holly and, to Holly's annoyance, nothing like so skinny.

'Did you see last night's episode?' asked Miranda. 'Wasn't it brilliant? How's he going to get out of *that* mess?'

Holly smiled, always pleased to see her best friend. 'Rocket boots, Jamie reckons,' she said.

'Rubbish!' said Miranda. 'He'll be wearing a bullet-proof vest.'

'That's exactly what I thought,' said Holly, secretly glad that Miranda hadn't come up with anything more interesting. It could be *very* irritating when Miranda came up with better solutions than she did. The same thing happened with the mystery books they both loved to read. They would both read the first half of a new book, and then they would write down their ideas for how things might

15

actually turn out. The one who came closer was the winner. Unless, of course, one of them came up with an idea that was actually *better* than how the book ended, and then they'd be Super Winner and Chief of All Detectives.

The two friends had different classes first thing that morning, so they agreed to meet up in the resource room at break.

It was in the resource room that they coedited the lower-school magazine, *The Tom-tom*. The title was Miranda's idea, linking Thomas Petheridge's name with the drums that people use for passing messages. *The Tom-tom* was published monthly. It was only a few photocopied pages, but Holly and Miranda were very proud of their work.

Holly dreamed of becoming a journalist as well as a spy. After all, she thought, you wouldn't last long if people asked you what you did for a living, and you told them you were a *spy*. It would be far better to be able to say, 'Oh, I'm a journalist, you know.'

Just like Superman! Quiet, mild-mannered Holly Adams works as a journalist by day, but as night falls, her true identity is revealed

16

as the Spy-catcher! A plague to all enemy agents!

One of the interesting new ideas Holly and Miranda had for the magazine was a mystery column. In it they would review all the new books they had read, as well as commenting on any mystery TV shows or films they had seen.

Miranda also edited a bad-jokes column, with jokes like:

Question: What do you call it when two dinosaurs crash into each other?
Answer: T. Wrecks.

Sometimes they spent more time groaning over the terrible jokes that people handed in than they did over the whole of the rest of the magazine. But it was always the mystery column that they enjoyed writing most.

As they worked on the magazine that morning, they chatted about the realities of becoming spy-catchers.

'For instance,' said Miranda, sucking the end of her pen. 'What qualifications do you need?'

'Sharp eyes,' said Holly. 'A fiendishly

17

clever mind. The ability to blend into the background. Stuff like that.'

'But how do you learn things like that?' asked Miranda.

'By practising,' said Holly. 'That's what we ought to do: practise a lot.' She sat back, gazing thoughtfully out of the window. 'We should set ourselves a project. That's what teachers always do when they want you to learn about something. Set a project.'

'Like what?' asked Miranda.

'I don't know,' said Holly. 'Like, following someone without being seen. Noting down everywhere they go. Keeping tabs on them and writing a full report of all their movements. Everyone they speak to. Everywhere they go.'

'Hmm,' said Miranda. 'Who, though? Who around here is interesting enough to be worth following?'

'Well,' said Holly. 'There's your mum, for a start. She works for the Government, doesn't she?'

'My mum isn't a secret agent!' said an astonished Miranda. 'She's just an ordinary civil servant. All she does is translate loads of boring foreign documents into English.'

'Exactly!' Holly said brightly. '*Foreign* documents. Who knows what sort of stuff she might get to see? All sorts of secret information, I bet! I'm surprised she doesn't have agents following her all over the place.'

Miranda grinned. 'They'd soon get sent packing if they did,' she said. 'I can't see my mum taking any nonsense from secret agents.' She let out a loud laugh. 'She'd just send them to bed without any supper!'

'A good agent wouldn't be *seen* though,' said Holly. 'That's the whole point of being a spy. They'd wait until there was no one about, then they'd use a skeleton key to get your mum's office door open at dead of night. They'd have a special camera to take photos of all the secret documents. *Click, click, click.* And then they'd slip quietly away to meet a private plane.' Holly smiled. 'And by breakfast time, photos of all the secret documents would be sitting on a desk somewhere in another country. *That's* how it's done.'

'Well,' said Miranda, 'there's not much we could do about that, is there?' Her eyes suddenly lit up. 'Unless someone tried to photograph stuff from Mum's filing cabinet at home.'

19

The Hunts' spare room was used by Miranda's parents as an office. When she had a rush job on, Miranda's mother often brought official files home and tapped away into the night at her word processor.

'That's it!' said Holly. 'That can be our project! Protecting your mum's stuff from intruders! We can work out an alarm system. We can go over to your house after school today. What do you say?'

'You're on!' said Miranda. 'Our first job! Hunt and Adams, spy-catchers!'

Holly looked at her with raised eyebrows. 'I thought "Adams and Hunt" sounded better,' she said.

'You would,' said Miranda. 'I prefer "Hunt and Adams". People will see the name "Hunt" first, and they'll think: *Oh, these people must be good at hunting for spies.* See?'

'Hmm,' said Holly, unconvinced. 'Perhaps we should think up something that doesn't have either of our names in it. What about "Spies-R-Us"? Something like that.'

'OK,' said Miranda. 'Spies-R-Us, it is.'

The bell sounded for the end of break.

Holly looked at the scattering of paper for

20

the magazine. 'Oops,' she said. 'We didn't get much done, did we?'

'We'll come back at lunch-time,' said Miranda. 'And this time we'll really concentrate on getting the magazine sorted out.'

The magazine had to be finished and photocopied by Friday morning, ready to be handed out before next week's half-term holiday.

It's very difficult, thought Holly as they tidied their work away, *it's* very *difficult trying to do two things at once.*

Especially when one of the things was as exciting as setting up their anti-spy agency!

21

The spider and the fly

'Hello! Anyone in?' Miranda yelled as the two friends stood in the Hunts' hall that afternoon. There was no response.

'Good,' said Miranda, throwing her school-bag against the wall. 'That means that Becky and Rachel aren't back yet, so there's no one to interfere.' Becky and Rachel were Miranda's twin fifteen-year-old sisters. Tall and thin, they reminded Holly of a pair of blonde-haired bookends. They were almost identical except for the fact that Rachel had short hair and Becky's nose was bigger.

Jamie might be a pest, Holly had often thought, but at least there was only one of him. And he was much smaller than her so she could always sit on him if he got too much. She couldn't imagine how Miranda coped with older twin sisters, constantly poking their noses into everything

22

she was doing. And they were so sarcastic with it.

Holly and Miranda went into the kitchen for a quick snack and a discussion about how they were going to set up an alarm system.

'We need something that will set off a bell,' said Miranda. 'So that when someone opens the door, an alarm will ring. Wires or something, attached to the door handle. They open the door and, *crash, bang, wallop!* The whole house is alerted.'

'Have you got a bell, then?' asked Holly.

'Well, no, not exactly,' admitted Miranda. 'But there's a reel full of fishing-line down in the cellar from when Dad used to go fishing. We could use that for wiring. We could run it along the wall and up the stairs into my room. And then we could attach it to something in there.'

'That's a lot of wire,' said Holly. 'How would you hold it in place?'

'Nails?' suggested Miranda. Her face dropped. 'Or perhaps not,' she said. 'Mum and Dad aren't going to be too amused if I bang nails in all over the place.' She frowned. 'This is going to be a lot more complicated than I'd thought.'

23

'Not necessarily,' said Holly. 'I've had a really good idea. Instead of setting up an alarm, why don't we arrange something to frighten people off?' She put her hand in her pocket and brought out a large, wobbly, black rubber spider. 'I borrowed this from Jamie,' she said. 'Imagine if you opened a door and *this* came flying at you.'

'I'd scream the place down,' Miranda said with a shudder as the rubber spider's red stalk-eyes wobbled menacingly at her.

'Exactly!' said Holly. 'All we need to do is pin it to the inside of the door frame on a bit of wire long enough for it to dangle at about head height. When someone pushes the door open, it'll come swinging out at them. I bet even the bravest spy would yell at that.'

'Holly, that's brilliant,' Miranda said in admiration.

'It's like my mum says,' Holly beamed. 'Simple things are always the best.'

'Have the last crisp,' said Miranda, holding out the packet. 'You deserve it. And then,' she said with a grin, 'we set our spy trap.'

The whole thing only took them half an hour. They cut a piece of fishing-line from

Mr Hunt's reel and attached it to the frame of the office door with the spider tied to the end.

When they tried it out, it worked perfectly. As Holly pushed the door open, the top of the door caught the line and stretched it out. She ducked as the spider came flopping over the top of the door and swung down over her head.

'Yuk!' said Miranda with a shiver as the spider swung to and fro in the doorway, its legs and eyes wobbling horribly. "That would give me the screaming heebie-jeebies.'

'All we need to do now,' said Holly, 'is to put another drawing-pin in, so we can hook the line up out of the way for when it's not needed.' She grinned. 'We don't want your mum or dad getting caught.' She pushed the spider back over the door and closed it. 'Brilliant!'

'I'll get another drawing-pin,' said Miranda. 'I've got some more in my room.'

Holly went upstairs with her.

'We should patent this idea,' said Holly. 'The Spies-R-Us Alarm System.'

'Spiders-R-Us!' said Miranda. 'Oh, rats!' she exclaimed. She kept her drawing-pins in

25

a small tin and, as she had picked it up, the lid had fallen open, sending pins cascading all over the floor. 'Don't move! You might step on one.' She crouched down, scooping the drawing-pins together.

'Can you see any I've missed?' she asked.

'There's one over by the bed,' said Holly. 'Hey, I've just thought of another anti-spy device. Drawing-pins scattered on the floor just inside the room. Even if someone wasn't afraid of spiders, they'd soon yell if they trod on a few drawing-pins.'

'They'd be wearing shoes,' said Miranda. 'They wouldn't feel them.'

'Oh, I suppose not,' said Holly. 'But you never know. If someone was prowling around in the dead of night, they might well take their shoes off.'

'Hmm,' said Miranda. 'I think we'll stick with the flying spider for the time being.'

They had been too busy up there to hear the front door opening and closing downstairs. The first they knew of anyone else having entered the house was when a fiendish scream came echoing up the stairs.

They stared at each other for a split second, then went tumbling out of Miranda's room, almost falling over each other as they rushed down the stairs.

The screams were still echoing around the house. Miranda's sister Rachel was in a heap on the hall carpet with her back to the wall and her legs stretched out. A plastic shopping bag was lying at her side, its contents spilling out over the floor. The door to the office room was open and the spider was swinging merrily on its thread, legs wobbling away as Rachel stared at it with her eyes almost popping out of her head.

'Calm down!' Miranda yelled above the piercing noise her sister was making. 'It's not *real*!'

Rachel stared at them, gasping for breath. 'What? You . . . you . . . *imbecile!*' she howled. 'You stupid, idiotic *moron*!' She picked herself up, trembling all over as she glared at the two friends. 'Was that supposed to be *funny*?' she yelled.

'It was supposed to be a trap for anyone going in there when they shouldn't!' shouted Miranda.

Rachel stared down at the spilled shopping. A bag of sugar had burst open and three

27

or four slimy broken eggs were spreading over the carpet.

'Look what you've done!' yelled Rachel. 'You wait till I tell Mum!'

'You wouldn't have been caught if you hadn't been poking your nose in there,' said Miranda. 'What were you doing, going in there anyway?'

'Mum said to put the receipt for the shopping on the memo board in there so it won't get lost,' said Rachel. 'I'm not taking the blame for this mess,' she said. She grabbed at the spider and wrenched it down, flinging it at Miranda. 'Idiot!' she yelled. 'You clean this up, and then you can go down to the shops and replace all the stuff you've ruined. *I'm* not doing it.'

She pulled her clothes straight and gave them a final glare as she stormed off towards the kitchen.

Holly and Miranda looked at each other.

Miranda gave a weak grin. 'Maybe it wasn't such a good idea after all,' she said, dangling the spider in front of Holly's face. 'Do you fancy coming to the shops with me?'

Holly bit her lip. 'She did *scream*, didn't

she?' she said, trying not to laugh. 'I mean, it *worked*, didn't it? Did you see her face?'

Miranda contorted her face into a replica of Rachel's horrified look and they both started giggling.

'I can hear you!' yelled Rachel from the kitchen. 'You'll have something else to laugh about when I tell Mum!'

'What did your mum say?' asked Holly when she met up with Miranda at school the next morning.

'She said it's not her office that needs protecting from burglars,' said Miranda. 'She said it's everyone else in the house that needs protecting from me.' She grinned. 'Well, from *us*, actually.'

'I'm in her bad books as well, am I?' asked Holly.

'Sort of,' said Miranda. 'I think we'd better forget about trying to do my mum any favours for a while.' She tossed her hair. 'It'd serve her right if the place got ransacked.'

'Did you tell her why we did it?' asked Holly. 'About spies trying to steal all her secret papers?'

'Of course I did,' said Miranda. 'She said

29

that if foreign agents were particularly interested in information about Belgian sewage
systems, then they were welcome to it,
because that was the only stuff they'd find
in there.'

Holly wrinkled her nose. 'Sewage systems?'

Miranda nodded. 'She said she never gets
any secret stuff to translate.' She gave Holly a
guilty smile. 'I think we'd better put Spies-R-
Us on hold for the time being, don't you?'

'I wouldn't say that,' said Holly. 'I've had
another idea.'

Miranda put her hands over her face. 'Oh,
no. Not *another* idea? I don't know if I could
cope with another of your ideas right now.'

'Don't panic,' said Holly. 'This one will
be really interesting.' She reached into her
school-bag. 'Look what I dug up.'

It was a book.

'*Harriet the Spy*!' said Miranda with a laugh.
'Gosh. I haven't read that for ages.'

The book was old and tattered, as both
Holly and Miranda had read it over and
over again when they had first bought it.
Their fascination with mysteries and spies
had all started with *Harriet the Spy*. Harriet

30

lived in America, in New York. She spent her free time wandering around, keeping a watch on all her neighbours and writing down all the details of their movements in a secret notebook.

Miranda took the book from Holly and flipped through a few pages, smiling as she remembered her favourite parts.

'Hold on, though,' she said. 'You're not suggesting we should start spying on our neighbours, are you? I don't want all the people in my street complaining to my mum.'

'That's not the idea at all,' said Holly. 'But what if I were to tell you about someone I've seen acting in a very suspicious way? A specific person who goes around all the time with a little booklet, and who seems to spend an awful lot of time scribbling stuff down in it?'

'Who?' asked Miranda. 'What sort of stuff?'

'I don't know,' said Holly. 'That's the whole point. I don't know what he keeps writing down. But I'd *like* to know. I've seen him three or four times recently.' She gave Miranda a conspiratorial smile. 'He would be the perfect target for our first investigation. Half-term's coming up, so we could spend all our free time on it. We could take it in turns to watch him. We could open a file on him. Find out where he lives. Find out what he's *doing.*'

Miranda looked dubiously at her. 'You're sure this won't get us into any trouble?' she said.

'There's always an element of risk if you're going to be a spy,' Holly said solemnly. 'But if we're clever, he won't even know he's being watched.'

'I don't know,' said Miranda, looking uneasily into her friend's excited eyes. '*Your* good ideas always seem to backfire on *me*. I don't want to spend half-term grounded because someone's complained to my parents.'

Holly fixed her with a steely look. 'Do you want to be a spy when you grow up, or do you want to spend your life stacking shelves in a supermarket?'

Miranda sighed. 'Are you giving me the choice?' she asked.

'Not really,' Holly said with a grin.

Miranda shrugged. When Holly was in this sort of mood, there wasn't really anything else a person could do but go along with her.

'OK,' said Miranda. 'I'm with you. Tell me all about it. Who exactly is this man we're going to be spying on?'

Holly lifted a finger. 'Meet me at the front gates after school, and I'll take you to where I've seen him,' she whispered. She glanced round. 'And remember,' she said. 'Not a word to anyone! Our mission depends on absolute secrecy!'

Miranda laughed. 'Holly,' she said. 'Has anyone ever told you you're completely potty?'

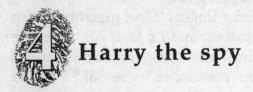

4 Harry the spy

'There he is,' whispered Holly. 'Harry the Spy!'

It was late afternoon the same day. Instead of their usual back-street route home, Holly had led Miranda towards the busy main streets. They came out into a street lined with shops and filled with slow-moving traffic. At one end, the traffic halted and gradually fed into a roundabout before heading off down several other streets. It was one of those places where there was always a lot of traffic waiting to get through.

Miranda followed the line of Holly's pointing finger. Sitting on a low wall near the roundabout was a boy in jeans and a denim jacket. He was thin, his brown hair hanging in his eyes as he stared at the tangle of cars and lorries. He looked about the same age as the two girls.

'It's a boy,' said Miranda.

'Well spotted,' said Holly. 'You get full marks for observation.'

Miranda frowned at her. 'I mean, it's *only* a boy,' she said. 'When you said you'd seen someone taking notes, I thought you meant a grown-up.'

The two girls stood in a shop doorway. Miranda peered at the boy, seeing how, every now and then, he would scribble something down in a small notebook before resuming his observation of the traffic.

'He's just collecting car number plates,' said Miranda. 'Boys do weird stuff like that.'

'That's what's so clever about it,' said Holly. 'That's exactly what everyone is *supposed* to think.'

Miranda looked at her. 'So what do you think he's really doing?'

'He's pretending to be taking car number plates,' said Holly. 'But *really*, he's watching for a *particular* car.'

'What sort of particular car?'

'I don't know yet,' said Holly. 'Maybe a car with an important diplomat in it. He could be on the lookout for a foreign power. Perhaps they're planning a kidnapping.'

35

'You're crackers,' said Miranda. 'Why would some foreign power use a *boy*?'

Holly gave her a superior look. 'To fool people like *you*,' she said. 'No one would be suspicious of a boy, would they? They'd all fall for it, just like you have.'

Miranda giggled.

'What's so funny?' asked Holly.

'Oh, nothing,' said Miranda. 'I mean, it's all so *obvious*, now you come to explain it to me. Of course he's working for a foreign power, Holly.' She patted her friend on the shoulder. 'Of *course* he is!' She giggled again.

'That's it, make fun,' said Holly. 'I bet everyone laughed at, um . . . ' Her voice trailed off.

'At who?'

'I don't know,' Holly said crossly. 'At someone who knew something suspicious was going on when no one else realised it.'

'Why did you call him Harry?' asked Miranda, giving the boy another quick look.

'That's the code-name I've given him,' explained Holly. 'You have to give everyone a code-name when you open a file on them.' She took a brand new notebook out of her

36

pocket and opened it to the first page. She showed it to Miranda. At the top of the blank page Holly had written: 'Code-name, Harry'.

'Now,' said Holly, taking out a pen, 'I write today's date.' She consulted her watch. 'The exact time, and the place where he's been seen.'

'Then what?' asked Miranda.

'We follow him,' said Holly.

'But he isn't going anywhere,' Miranda pointed out.

'No, but he *will*,' said Holly. 'He's not going to sit there forever, is he?'

Miranda sucked her lips in, trying not to laugh.

Holly glared at her. 'You're not taking this seriously, are you?' she said crossly.

'Well, come on, Holly,' said Miranda with a wide grin. 'I'd feel like a complete idiot following him about. He's about as likely to be involved in a plot to kidnap an important diplomat as I am to be planning a bank robbery. He's just an ordinary boy, doing the sort of dozy things that ordinary boys *always* do.'

Holly's eyebrows knitted. 'Just answer me this,' she said. 'Do you want to be my partner in Spies-R-Us?'

37

'Yes, of course,' said Miranda.

'Then get this into your head,' Holly said firmly. 'This is a training exercise. Get it? It doesn't *matter* whether he's taking number plates or not. It doesn't matter *what* he's doing.'

Miranda's eyes lit up as she finally understood.

'Ohhh,' she said. 'You're only pretending!' Her face split in a wide grin. 'I thought for a minute there that you really *believed* all that stuff about diplomats getting kidnapped.'

'So, are we going to watch him or not?' asked Holly.

'Yes,' said Miranda. 'I get it now.' She looked across at the boy. 'How long do we have to watch him for?'

'Until we get all the information we need,' said Holly. 'It could take a few days.'

'I don't really fancy spending the whole of our half-term holiday trailing around after some *boy*,' said Miranda. She laughed. 'My sisters do enough of that. Ow! Holly, don't grab me like that!'

Holly's fingers had closed suddenly around her arm.

'He's moving,' hissed Holly. 'Look!'

The boy had got up from the low wall and was walking away from them.

'Good,' said Miranda. 'Does that mean we can go home now?'

'No. We've got to follow him,' said Holly, dragging Miranda along behind her.

'OK, let go,' said Miranda. 'I'm coming.'

There were a lot of afternoon shoppers about. Holly had to dodge past them to keep the boy in sight. He was ambling along with his head lowered.

Holly smiled in that particular way she had seen Secret Agent John Raven smile when he was hot on someone's trail.

The boy came to a halt at the kerb, waiting along with a lot of other people for the traffic lights to change. Holly glanced round at Miranda, intending to warn her not to get too close to the boy. 'Miranda! What are you playing at?'

Behind Holly's back, Miranda had buttoned her jacket to her throat, and pulled the collar up. And she had put on a pair of dark glasses.

'How did you know it was me?' said Miranda with a grin. 'I'm in disguise. What do you think? Pretty cool, huh?'

'Are you completely mad?' Holly whispered. 'It's not even sunny!'

Miranda took the dark glasses off. 'I'm only trying to get into the swing of things,' she said. 'I thought people like us *always* wore dark glasses, so we wouldn't be recognised.'

'You'll be recognised, all right,' said Holly. 'No one's going to forget what *you* look like, you twit!' She glanced at the boy and was horrified to see that he was staring straight at them.

She ducked down to a crouch.

'What are you doing?' asked Miranda.

'Pretending to tie my shoelace,' whispered Holly. 'He's looking this way. Do something innocent-looking.'

Miranda pushed her hands into her pockets and started whistling loudly as she gazed into the air with the most innocent look on her face that she could manage.

Holly groaned. Miranda might just as well have had a neon sign strapped to her head, beaming out, *I Am Behaving Suspiciously!*

The traffic lights changed and people began to cross the road. Holly stood up.

'How was I?' asked Miranda.

'Hopeless,' said Holly. 'Come on, or we'll lose him.'

They crossed the road and followed the boy along the pavement. Holly had to keep yanking Miranda back to keep a few metres distance between them and the boy.

Twice he glanced over his shoulder. Both times, Holly pulled Miranda over to a shop window and pretended to be showing her something.

'Do you think he's on to us?' whispered Miranda. 'He keeps looking back.'

The boy looked round again, then made a sudden movement across the pavement and disappeared into a narrow alley between two shops.

'Where's he gone?' asked Miranda, who'd been too busy looking in the shop windows to see the boy go.

'Down there,' said Holly, pointing to the alley. 'Now, this is where we find out just how good we are at trailing people. I'll keep after him. You double back down that sidestreet and catch him on his way out. But don't let him *see* you.'

'This is fun,' said Miranda, turning and running back towards the sidestreet.

41

Holly wasn't at all sure Miranda had the right attitude for this. Spy-catchers weren't supposed to think it was *fun*!

Holly looked down the alley. Her eyes widened. In those few seconds the boy had vanished completely. But what was even weirder was the fact that the alley was a dead-end. There was no way out. It was as if the alley had simply swallowed him up.

Puzzled, Holly began to walk down the alley.

She nearly jumped out of her skin as she saw the boy leaning casually against a shallow doorway in the alley's wall.

He looked at her, a faint smile on his face.

'Lost?' he asked, still smiling.

'No,' gasped Holly. 'I mean – yes! Yes, I am.' Her brain raced in several different directions as the boy's brown eyes looked quizzically at her. 'Could you tell me the way to Griebler Road?'

'I'm afraid not,' said the boy. 'I don't know this area very well.'

'Oh.' Holly gave him a sheepish grin.

'I don't think you'll find it down here,' said the boy, glancing meaningfully at the dead-end.

Holly suddenly felt very hot. She was sure she was blushing. Something about the way the boy was looking at her made her feel as if he knew exactly what she was up to.

'Oh, well,' she said. 'I'd better ask someone else. Thanks anyway.'

'You're welcome,' said the boy.

Holly turned round sharply, nearly colliding with Miranda as she came cannoning around the corner.

'There's no way out . . . *oh!*' Miranda's mouth fell open as she saw the boy. 'Oh. I, er—'

'Excuse me,' interrupted Holly. 'I'm afraid I'm *lost*.' She stared Miranda into baffled silence. 'Could you tell me the way to Griebler Street?'

Miranda gave her an anxious look.

'I think you mean Griebler *Road*, don't you?' said the boy. He detached himself from the doorway and walked past them towards the mouth of the alley. There was no mistaking the amused look on his face as he glanced back at them before going around the corner and out of sight.

'Why did you ask me that?' said Miranda.

43

'I didn't want him to realise we knew each other,' said Holly.

'But he'd seen us together,' said Miranda. 'He must think we're crackers.'

'I panicked,' Holly admitted unhappily. 'Do you think he's on to us?'

'Never in a million years,' said Miranda. Her ringing laughter echoed around the alley. 'Some spies *we* are!'

Supermarket spies

'Are you sure we're really cut out to be spies?' asked Miranda. 'Perhaps we ought to think about becoming a comedy double act instead? Adams and Hunt: Clowns-R-Us!'

They stood in the narrow alley. The memory of the boy's amused smile made Holly's cheeks burn.

'It's not funny,' Holly said. 'I feel a total fool!'

'Don't worry about it,' Miranda said cheerfully. 'You can't win them all.'

'But this was our first assignment,' complained Holly. 'And look at the mess we made of it.' She groaned. 'We can't even follow a stupid *boy* without getting caught out.'

'He's not stupid,' Miranda said thoughtfully. 'He sussed us out pretty quickly. He didn't come down this alley by accident. He

45

did it to trap us.' She grinned. 'He's a better spy-catcher than *we* are.'

'Yes. Thanks. That's cheered me up no end,' said Holly. 'Is my face still red?'

'Like a beetroot,' said Miranda. 'What *was* all that about Griebler Street? I've never heard of it.'

'It was the only thing I could think of,' said Holly. 'The Grieblers are my next-door neighbours. It might have worked if you hadn't just stood there with your mouth hanging open.'

'Face it,' said Miranda. 'We're rotten spies.' Her face suddenly lit up and she let out a loud laugh.

'Now what?' said Holly.

'I just thought of a great joke for the magazine,' said Miranda. 'What do you call people who spy on sheep?'

'I don't know,' said Holly, in no mood for Miranda's bad jokes.

'Shepherd spies!' said Miranda. 'Get it? Shepherds' pies!' She looked into Holly's gloomy face. 'Oh, cheer up, can't you? It's not the end of the world. So we made one mistake. We can soon find someone else to follow.'

Holly stared down at the ground. Her expression changed as she spotted a slip of paper in the doorway where the boy had been standing. She walked over and picked it up.

'Look,' she said. 'He must have dropped it.'

'Don't be daft,' said Miranda. '*Anyone* could have dropped it. It could have been there ages.'

'But it's clean,' said Holly. 'And it's dry. It was raining earlier. It would be all soggy if it had been here for any length of time.' She turned the slip of paper over. 'And it's been torn from a notebook the same size as the one he was using,' she said.

'Is there anything written on it?' asked Miranda.

'Yes. An address,' said Holly. 'Look! "241 High Street".' She looked at Miranda. '*That*'s High Street,' she said, pointing out of the alley.

'OK,' said Miranda. 'Let's go and see what's at number 241.'

They came out into the main street. There was no sign of the boy on the busy pavement. Holly looked up at the street numbers.

47

'160,' she read. '158. So 241 will be on the other side, in *that* direction.'

'Come on then,' said Miranda, heading for the crossing. 'This is one bit of sleuthing we *can't* get wrong.'

They stood in front of number 241 High Street. It was a health-food shop. Above the window was a sign: *The Nut House*.

Miranda looked at Holly.

'Do you think he's trying to tell us something?' she said, holding back a smile.

Holly's eyes narrowed. 'OK, *boy*,' she said. 'You think you're clever, do you? We'll see just how clever you are! No one makes a fool of Holly Adams and gets away with it. I'm going to find out every last thing about you. Every detail.'

'Careful,' warned Miranda. 'He's pretty sharp.'

Holly glared at her. 'And so am I!' she said. 'So am I.'

They saw no sign of the boy again that week, despite the fact that Holly insisted on dragging Miranda off to the High Street after school each day. The low wall by the roundabout remained empty.

48

On Friday afternoon, Miranda finally lost patience with Holly. 'I'm fed up with this,' she told Holly. 'I'm going home. Are you coming?'

'No,' Holly said. 'I'm going to get revenge on that boy. I don't care how long it takes.'

Miranda went home without her, leaving Holly to watch the empty wall on her own. Holly hung around for half an hour before giving up.

She didn't like being made to look silly. It was a point of honour with her that she should somehow get her own back on the boy. But how? She didn't know the first thing about him. She didn't even know where he lived or what school he went to. She didn't even know his name.

By the weekend, even Holly had to admit she was beaten.

Sunday afternoon in the Adams house was usually a relatively peaceful time.

Holly was lying on the couch in the living room, reading her mystery book, *The Claws of the Cat*. At least in books everything worked out right. The villains might lead the hero a merry dance for a while, but at

49

least you know that the hero will win in the end.

If she got the chance to *get* to the end. Jamie and a couple of friends were occupying most of the floor space, playing a board game that involved a lot of yelling and fighting. Hammerings and sawings and the sound of an electric lathe drifted up from the cellar. Mr Adams was busy with his hobby.

'Can't you play that somewhere else?' complained Holly, glaring at her brother. 'I'm trying to read.'

'Can't you *read* somewhere else?' said Jamie. 'We were here first. Hoy! Martin, I *saw* that, you big cheat!'

Holly sighed. There was obviously not going to be any peace down here. She picked up her book and took herself out into the hall, intending to go up to the quiet of her room.

She saw her mother sitting at the kitchen table, frowning over a heap of documents. The thought of a mid-afternoon snack cheered Holly up a bit, and she went through to the kitchen.

'Busy?' she asked her mother.

Mrs Adams gave her a frazzled look. 'It's the new manager,' she said. 'He's changing

50

all the routines. I don't know whether I'm coming or going.' Mrs Adams worked in a local bank. She was the head of her own department. Holly had heard her complaining before about the new man who had taken over as manager of the bank. His name was Mr Cheevers, Holly remembered.

'Is he no good then?' asked Holly, her head inside the fridge in search of something nice to eat.

'I expect he knows what he's doing,' sighed Mrs Adams. 'The problem is, no one *else* knows what he's doing. He's only been there three weeks, and – Holly? What are you looking for?'

'Something to nibble,' said Holly.

'There's a packet of peanuts in the cupboard,' said Mrs Adams.

'Ooh. That'll do nicely,' Holly said with a grin. 'There's not much interesting in the fridge.'

'I know,' said her mother. 'I didn't get a chance to do much shopping last week.'

'But it's half-term,' said Holly. 'Haven't you got any treats in?'

'No. Sorry,' said Mrs Adams. 'I'll tell you what, though. I'll give you some money in the morning and you and Jamie can go down to the supermarket for me.'

Holly's face registered instant dismay.

'I'd rather ask Miranda,' she said.

'OK,' said Mrs Adams. 'I'll make you out a list. Now, can you leave me in peace, Holly? I've got to try to make sense of this lot by tomorrow morning.'

Holly took the packet of peanuts out of the cupboard and went upstairs for a quiet hour or so with her book.

'Oh, wow!' said Miranda. 'You take me to the *nicest* places, Holly.'

It was Monday morning in the local supermarket. With the shopping money carefully folded away in her pocket and her mother's list in one hand, Holly marched ahead while Miranda followed with a trolley.

'No need to thank me,' said Holly, dumping a bag of potatoes in the trolley and ticking them off the list.

'I was being sarcastic,' mumbled Miranda. 'Have you got ice cream on that list?'

'Yes.'

'Oh,' Miranda's face brightened. 'That's not so bad then. Strawberry?'

'Chocolate,' said Holly. She smiled round at her friend. 'But we can make it strawberry.' Her voice trailed off as she stared at something way past Miranda's shoulder.

Miranda looked round. 'What?' she asked.

'That *boy*,' said Holly. 'It's *him*!'

Holly was staring over towards the corner of the supermarket set aside for magazines.

'Where?' asked Miranda. 'I can't see him.'

'He's gone now,' said Holly. 'I only caught a glimpse of him. But it was *him*. I'm sure of it. I recognised his hair, and the black jacket.'

'His jacket was blue, wasn't it?' said Miranda.

Holly gave her a scathing look. '*Black*,' she insisted. 'Some witness you'd make!'

'I'll bet you it was blue,' said Miranda.

'You're on,' said Holly. 'Loser has to carry all the heaviest stuff, right?'

'Fine by me,' said Miranda. 'Which way did he go?' She spun the trolley round, almost knocking a couple of people over. 'Sorry,' she said. 'Oops! Sorry. Excuse me! Mind your backs, please. Express trolley coming through!'

'Miranda! For heaven's sake!' said Holly, as

her friend cut a path through the shoppers. 'You'll run someone over.'

Miranda swerved the trolley round a corner, making a noise like a police siren: 'Nee-nah, nee-nah, nee-nah!'

'Miranda! Stop showing me up!' hissed Holly. 'We'll get thrown out!'

Miranda's trolley went trundling up an aisle.

'I'll go this way,' called Holly. 'See you at the other end.' She backed out of the aisle and began to walk along the ends of the aisles, her eyes roving about for another sight of the mysterious boy.

She pushed her way through the queue of people at the delicatessen counter. Could she have been mistaken?

No! There he was again. Right at the far end of the row of aisles. And he was looking straight at her.

The boy grinned, lifting his hand to give her a little wave before ducking out of sight. Holly shoved her way determinedly through the bottle-neck of shoppers. He was taunting her! Of all the cheek!

She glanced along each aisle, hoping for a sight of Miranda as she ran along.

'No running in here, please,' said a man in a brown suit with a clipboard in his hand. 'This isn't a playground.'

'Sorry,' said Holly, slowing down and giving him an apologetic smile.

She was about to pass him when she heard a crash from somewhere up ahead. The crash of falling cans and a shriek.

Only one person in the world had a shriek like that. Miranda.

'Now what?' exclaimed the man, walking briskly towards where the noise had come from.

Holly followed him. She could see it all! Miranda and her out-of-control trolley! Perhaps it might have been better if Jamie had come with her after all.

She trailed the man around a corner. She saw the chaos at the far end of the aisle and put her hands over her eyes.

It was Miranda all right.

A new recruit

Astonished shoppers were spreading away from the disaster area as cans rolled among their feet. An entire display pyramid had been demolished. Baked beans. A huge tower of baked-bean cans. And sitting in the middle of all the chaos were Miranda and the boy in the denim jacket.

The shop man marched up to them.

Miranda stood up, her arms windmilling as a can rolled under her foot.

'Ouch!' she said, rubbing herself. Holly gave her an agonised look over the man's shoulder.

'What's going on here?' said the man.

The boy swept his hair out of his eyes and peered up into the man's angry face.

'If you don't mind me saying so,' said the boy, picking himself up, 'that's a really stupid place to put such an unstable stack of cans.

56

Someone might have been hurt.'

'Someone *was* hurt,' said Miranda. She caught sight of Holly and waved. Holly tried to hide behind the shop man's back.

'You were right,' Miranda called happily. 'His jacket *is* black!'

'I have never been so embarrassed in my entire life,' said Holly as the three of them stood on the forecourt outside the supermarket. The shop man had relieved Miranda of her trolley and had ordered all three of them out of the shop.

'It was an accident,' said Miranda, pointing at the boy. 'He ran straight into me.'

'Don't blame me,' said the boy. 'You must have been doing about eighty kilometres an hour with that trolley.'

'You should have been watching where you were going!' said Miranda. 'I bet I'm going to be covered in bruises. Those cans are really hard.'

'It serves you right,' said the boy. He looked at Holly. 'It serves *both* of you right. Perhaps you'll think twice before following people around in future.'

'I don't know what you're talking about,'

said Holly in as dignified a way as she could manage. 'What makes you think we'd waste our time following you around?'

The boy laughed, but not in an unkind way. Holly thought he had quite a nice face. 'I *saw* you staring at me the other day, and scribbling stuff down in that notebook,' he said. 'Who do you think you are, Harriet the Spy?'

Holly gaped at him. 'You know about *Harriet the Spy*?'

'I read it years ago,' said the boy with a grin. 'I remember she went around making notes about everyone. Just like you were doing last week. By the way, did you find my message?'

'Directing us to The Nut House,' said Miranda. 'Yes, we did.' She laughed. 'Holly wasn't very amused; were you, Holly?'

Holly looked carefully at him. 'Were we really that obvious?' she said.

'I wasn't sure until I lured you down that alley,' he said. 'Then I *knew* you were up to something.' He smiled. 'Come on, then, what was it all about?'

'Holly thought you were working as a spy,' said Miranda. 'She thought you were on the lookout for a car with a diplomat in it. She thought there was going to be a kidnapping.'

'I thought nothing of the sort!' exclaimed Holly, glaring at Miranda's smiling face. 'We were – it was . . . oh! All right, I admit it, we were taking notes about you. It was a sort of training exercise.'

'Training for what?' asked the boy.

'Holly wants to be a spy when she leaves school,' said Miranda.

'Thank *you*,' said Holly. 'Tell him all about it, why don't you?'

'A spy?' said the boy. 'Hey, I'm impressed.'

Holly looked narrowly at him. 'Are you being funny?' she asked.

He shook his head. 'Not at all,' he said. 'But if you want to be a spy, I think you could have found someone a bit more interesting to spy on. Why pick me?'

'I saw you watching the traffic and writing stuff down,' explained Holly.

'I collect number plates,' said the boy.

'What did I tell you?' crowed Miranda. 'I said that all along, didn't I? I told you he wasn't spying!'

'Will you shut up about that?' said Holly.

'I never did think he was a spy.'

'You just thought I was worth following, eh?' said the boy.

'What's your name?' asked Miranda. 'I'm Miranda Hunt, and this is Holly Adams.' She grinned. 'She's quite *normal* once you get to know her.'

'I wish I could say the same for you,' said Holly.

'I'm Peter. Peter Hamilton,' said the boy. 'My dad and I only just moved in around here. We live in Boxall Road.'

'That's only round the corner from me,' said Miranda. 'Do you live in one of those big houses?'

'No,' said Peter. 'We're in a flat in the estate on the other side of the road. It's only temporary, until Dad can find us a house.'

'You and your dad?' asked Miranda. 'Where's your mum, then?'

'Miranda!' said Holly. 'You're so nosey!'

'That's OK,' said Peter. He gave a small shrug, his face taking on an unhappy look. 'My mum died when I was only a kid. I don't really remember her.'

Miranda gave him an anxious look. 'Oh, I'm sorry. Me and my big mouth!'

'Don't worry about it,' said Peter. 'I'm sort of used to the idea.'

There was an awkward silence for a few moments. Peter's revelation about his mother had rather taken the wind out of the girls' sails.

'I've still got all that shopping to do,' sighed Holly. She glared at Miranda. 'And I can't go back in there now. Thanks to you.'

'Thanks to *him*,' said Miranda, pointing at Peter. She gave him a puzzled look. 'Excuse me for asking,' she said, 'but why do you collect car number plates?'

'It's interesting,' said Peter.

'It *is*?' said Miranda. 'In what way?'

'Well, you can work out how old cars are from the letter that's in with the numbers,' explained Peter. 'And then you can make up a chart to show how many cars there are from a particular year. At the moment I'm working on 1992.' Peter spoke animatedly, not seeming to notice as Miranda's eyes glazed over. 'And then there are foreign number plates,' he continued. 'I've got a special chart for them on the computer.'

'You've got your own computer?' said Holly.

'It's my dad's word-processor really, but he lets me use it whenever I like,' said Peter. 'Anyway, like I was saying—'

'Gosh!' interrupted Miranda, looking pointedly at her watch. 'Is that the time?'

Peter laughed. 'You did ask,' he said. He looked at them. 'I knew I shouldn't have bothered explaining,' he said. 'Girls can never understand stuff like that.'

This maddened Holly. 'What's that supposed to mean?' she said. 'Are you suggesting girls aren't bright enough?'

'It's nothing to do with being bright, especially,' said Peter. 'Girls just don't have the patience you need to sort through all the information.'

'Maybe girls are too bright to bother,' said Miranda. 'It sounds like a total waste of time, if you ask me.'

'You wouldn't say that if you'd spotted what I spotted the other day,' said Peter, apparently unconcerned by the annoyed expressions on the two girls' faces.

'Oh, do tell,' said Miranda. 'What was it? A really *exciting* number plate?'

'What would you say,' began Peter, 'if you saw a car with a particular number plate one day.' He looked sharply at them. 'And then saw the same car a couple of days later with a completely different number?'

'I'd say you needed glasses,' said Miranda.

Peter frowned at her. 'And you're supposed to be a trainee spy!' he said. 'For your information, I don't need glasses. And I didn't write the number down wrong, either. I saw the car in the carpark behind our flats last Friday. A white Ford Cortina with a dented rear bumper. It was gone over the weekend, and then it reappeared this morning. But with *different* number plates.' He pulled his notebook out of his jacket pocket. 'You can check the numbers if you don't believe me,' he said, flicking through crumpled pages filled with little neatly written rows of numbers.

'See!' he said, waving the notebook in Miranda's face. 'I've circled it in red. And here,' he said, turning over a couple of pages, 'is the number plate of the same car as I wrote it down this morning. See?'

'OK, OK,' said Miranda. 'Don't shove it up my nose. I can see. So what? I suppose people are entitled to change their number plates if they feel like it.'

'I don't think they are,' said Holly. She looked at Peter. 'Are they?'

'No,' said Peter. 'The only reason I can think of for anyone wanting to switch number plates is if the car was stolen.'

'Have you told the police?' asked Holly.

Peter gave her a strange look. 'No,' he said. 'I thought I'd keep an eye on it for a while. My bedroom window overlooks the carpark.' He grinned at them. 'I'm going to take photos of anyone who goes near the car.'

Holly's eyes lit up. 'You're going to keep watch on it?' she said. 'And then take photos of the thieves to the police? Is that it?'

'That's the plan,' said Peter.

'Then you're very lucky you've met us,' said Holly.

Peter looked dubiously at her. 'Am I? Why?'

'Because we can help,' said Holly, ignoring the look of dismay on Miranda's face. 'That's exactly the sort of training exercise we need.' She looked encouragingly at Miranda. 'It'd be much more interesting than just following people at random. I mean, we might actually be helping to catch some crooks. We could work together.'

'Excuse me,' said Miranda. 'Could I have a quiet word with you, Holly?' She frowned at Peter. 'In private.'

Peter shrugged and wandered off across the supermarket carpark, pen and notebook in hand.

'That was a bit rude,' said Holly.

'Never mind about that,' said Miranda, glancing over to where Peter was busy writing down number plates. 'I thought we were partners. We don't need *him*. You know what boys are like. Give him five minutes and he'll take over. He'll have us fetching drinks and making sandwiches before we know *where* we are.'

'No, he won't,' Holly said with a laugh. 'Knowing you, it'll be him who has to fetch drinks, if anyone does. Look, what if he's right? What if the car really is stolen and we can be in on finding out who stole it? It'd be great.'

'I'm not so sure,' said Miranda.

'Trust me,' said Holly. 'Just this once.'

'Just this *once*?' said Miranda. 'Holly, you're *always* saying that.'

'And have I ever let you down?'

Miranda stared at her. 'All the time.'

65

Holly let out a big sigh. 'OK. But trust me *this* time. Please? One last time?'

'All right,' said Miranda reluctantly. 'But the moment he suggests I put the kettle on, I'm out of there, right?'

'Right,' said Holly. She linked arms with Miranda. 'Come on,' she said. 'Let's go and find out some more about this car.'

7 The mysterious car

'Anyone fancy a drink?' asked Peter.

They were standing in a shadowed doorway at the back of the block of flats where Peter lived. A tarmac area spread out in front of them, bordered by steep grassy banks and surrounded by more red-brick blocks that formed the housing estate.

There were about half a dozen cars parked on the tarmac. Peter had pointed out a white, four-door car over in one corner. The Ford Cortina with the dented rear bumper, which Peter was convinced had been given false number plates over the previous weekend.

Peter noticed the look that passed between the two girls when he mentioned the drinks.

'There's a shop around the corner,' he said. 'I could go and get us some cans, if anyone's thirsty.'

67

'See!' Holly said to Miranda, feeling in the pocket of her jeans for some change.

'See what?' asked Peter.

'Nothing,' said Miranda, handing over some money. 'I'll have a cherry-cola, if they've got one.'

Peter took their money and pushed through the doors into the corridor that led to the front of the block.

Holly smiled at Miranda. 'He's OK, isn't he?'

'He passed the first test,' said Miranda. 'We'll see about the rest.' She folded her arms and leaned in the doorway, staring out at the white car.

'Just tell me one thing,' said Miranda. 'Why *exactly* are we standing here looking at this car?'

'We're observing,' said Holly. 'That's what secret agents do. Observe.'

'What do you think it's going to do? Sprout wings and fly away?' asked Miranda.

'When Peter gets back,' Holly said patiently, 'we'll take some photographs and write down all the details of what Peter saw.'

'What he *thinks* he saw,' said Miranda.

'What he *saw*,' insisted Holly. 'And there

might be something inside the car that could give us some clues.'

'So why don't we go over and have a closer look?' asked Miranda.

'Let's wait until Peter gets back,' said Holly.

'Why?' asked Miranda. 'Is he in charge, all of a sudden?'

'No.'

'Well, then!' said Miranda. 'You can stay here if you like, but I'm going to take a closer look.' She grinned at Holly. 'There'll probably be a *body* in the back. The previous owner, lying there with his legs in the air and his tongue hanging out.' Miranda gave Holly a look of gruesome relish. 'And a huge carving-knife sticking out of his shirt.'

'You'd be the first to scream your head off if there was,' said Holly. 'Come on then, if you must. Let's go and look.'

The two girls came out of the doorway and walked across towards the car.

'If it *is* stolen,' said Miranda, 'what's it doing here? Why would the thieves just leave it standing about?'

'Perhaps they're waiting for a buyer,' said Holly. 'Perhaps they've already got a buyer and the car is just waiting here to be picked up. I mean, they've got to put it *somewhere*, haven't they?'

'Or maybe,' said Miranda, 'it's already *been* bought. Maybe the person who bought it lives here.'

Holly looked nervously around at all the many staring windows.

'Maybe they're watching us right now,' said Miranda. 'Maybe there's a rifle trained on us at this very moment.' She made a sudden jump at Holly. '*Bang!*' she shouted as Holly nearly leaped out of her shoes.

'Don't *do* that!' gasped Holly.

'Holly's a scaredy-cat!' sang Miranda with a yell of laughter. Still laughing, she walked up to the car and stooped to peer through the windows. 'Aw, pity,' she said, grinning round at Holly. 'No dead body.'

'No anything at all,' said Holly, walking around the car and looking in through all the windows. She twisted her neck in the hope of spotting something between the seats or in the shelf under the dashboard, but the inside of the car was quite clean and bare. There wasn't even a road-map, or any of those odd little mascot things that people often attach to their mirrors.

'The petrol gauge is at zero,' said Miranda, using her hand to shield the sunlight from the glass.

'Of course it is,' said Holly. 'Don't you know *anything*? None of the dials register unless the car is turned on.'

'Don't they?' said Miranda. 'The clock seems to be at the right time.'

'That's different,' said Holly.

'Is it? How?' asked Miranda.

'I don't know,' said Holly. 'It just is.'

'But you just said—'

'Don't be so silly,' interrupted Holly. 'What's the use of a clock that stops every time you switch the car off?' She circled round to the back of the car and crouched down. 'Aha!' she said.

Miranda followed her round. '*Aha*? What sort of *aha*?'

'The sort of *aha* that you say when you spot something suspicious,' said Holly. 'Look at this!'

Miranda crouched next to her. Holly was pointing at the number plate.

Miranda stared at it for a few moments. 'Aha!' she said hopefully.

'You see it?' said Holly.

'No,' admitted Miranda. 'I don't see anything.'

'So why did you say *aha*?' asked Holly, frowning at her.

Miranda gave a sheepish grin. 'I thought it might help. What am I supposed to be looking at?'

'The dirt and rust,' said Holly.

Miranda looked again. The lower part of the back of the car was spotted all over with grimy rust patches.

'So they didn't look after it very well,' said Miranda. 'So what?'

'Look at the screws holding the number plate in place,' said Holly. 'They're all shiny. They must be brand-new. And *that*,' she said triumphantly, 'proves that Peter was right. The number plates *have* been switched recently.'

'Hey!' The two girls started at the sudden shout. 'Hey! What are you up to down there?'

In her shock, Holly found herself sitting on the tarmac. She scrambled to her feet. Miranda pulled herself up on Holly's arm and the two of them stood staring at the man who had shouted at them.

72

Holly made a mental note of his appearance. He was wearing a navy-blue suit and a red tie. He had a round puffy face and black hair that was going thin on top. His shirt front strained over a pot-belly. In one hand he held a large brown envelope. As he strode towards them, Holly noticed that he had a splay-footed kind of walk. Almost a waddle. His face was angry, and his thick eyebrows lowered over brown, red-rimmed eyes.

He blustered up to them. 'What are you doing to that car?' he asked. 'I saw you!'

'We weren't doing anything,' said Miranda. 'There's no law against looking, is there?'

'Don't use that tone of voice on me, my girl,' said the man. 'Now then, what's the game, eh? Why aren't you in school?'

'It's half-term,' said Holly, before Miranda got the chance to say something that would annoy the man even more. 'We're just waiting for a friend, that's all.' She thought quickly. 'I dropped a coin,' she said. 'I think it rolled under your car.'

The man's expression changed. 'This isn't my car,' he said. His red-rimmed eyes swivelled down to the ground. 'Have you found the coin?'

Holly crouched down again. 'I think I can see it,' she said, stretching out an arm under the back of the car. 'Yes! Here it is!' She stood up, her hand clenched, pretending to be holding a coin. 'Got it! Come on, Miranda.' She slid her hand under Miranda's arm and towed her away.

'You shouldn't hang around carparks,' the man shouted after them. 'You should have better things to do with your time.'

'What a cheek!' exclaimed Miranda. 'The nosey old so-and-so.'

'Shh! He'll hear you,' said Holly.

'I don't care if he does,' Miranda said loudly, twisting round in Holly's grip. 'I don't care if he *does*!'

'Miranda!' Holly dragged her towards the sheltered doorway at the back of the flats. 'You're showing me up again.'

'I hate nosey people,' said Miranda. She raised her voice again. 'Especially nosey people who walk like *ducks*!'

Holly pulled her through the doors. In the shelter of the sunken doorway, Holly turned and looked out through the wire-glass panels.

Miranda pulled her arm free. 'I've a good

mind to go back out there and tell him to mind his own business!'

'Wait!' said Holly. 'Look!'

The man had been standing at the back of the car, watching them walk away. Holly saw him staring at the doorway.

'Rats!' she said. 'He can see us. Come on, let's get out of sight.' She pulled Miranda along the hallway.

'Hello,' said Peter, shoving his way through the front doors with three cans of drink in his hands. 'They didn't have cherry-cola, so I got you – um, what are you doing?' He looked in confusion at the two girls as they pressed against the wall.

'Can you see the man by the car?' said Holly.

'What man?' Peter stepped towards the glass-panelled back door. Holly grabbed him and dragged him out of sight.

'Don't let him see you,' Holly whispered. 'We were having a look at the car and he came up and yelled at us.'

'Why didn't you wait for me?' asked Peter.

'What difference would that have made?' demanded Miranda. 'Is he still there?'

Peter edged along the wall and glanced

around the side of the glass panel. 'I can't see anyone,' he said.

Holly let out a breath. 'He must have gone.'

Peter looked out. 'Blue suit?' he said, 'Carrying a big envelope?'

'That's him,' said Holly.

'He's walking away from the car,' Peter told them. 'Down towards the other side of the block. No. Wait. He's stopped.'

'What's he doing now?' hissed Holly.

'Just standing there,' said Peter. 'He's looking around.'

'He's probably looking for some other people to bother!' said Miranda.

'No. He's turned round,' said Peter. 'He's walking back towards the car.' Peter slid to the side of the door. 'He's at the car,' he said. 'He's feeling in his pocket.' He ducked back. 'He's looking round.'

Holly peered cautiously around Peter's shoulder. 'He's opening the boot,' she exclaimed. 'And he said it wasn't his car!'

'Is there a dead body in there?' asked Miranda.

Peter stared at her. 'A *what*?'

'He's putting the envelope in the boot,' said

76

Holly. As she watched from cover, the man threw the large envelope into the boot and slammed it closed. She dived out of sight as his eyes swept the area.

'He's coming this way!' said Peter.

'Run for it!' gasped Holly. 'We mustn't let him see us!'

They ran higgledy-piggledy along the hallway.

Holly's mind raced faster than her feet. What was the strange man doing? Why had he told them the car wasn't his? What possible reason could he have for lying like that? And what was in the envelope?

8 Stake-out

They ran breathlessly up the zigzag stairway.

'Why are we running?' panted Miranda. 'We haven't done anything.'

Peter came to a skidding halt on the second-floor landing. He looked at Holly. 'Why *are* we running?' he asked.

'We don't want him to know we saw him,' said Holly. 'We need to go somewhere and have a proper discussion about this.'

Peter pushed the swing-doors open. 'We can talk in my flat,' he said.

He fished out his keys and let them into the flat. Holly was struck by how neat and bare everything looked. There were no ornaments or pictures on the walls. It looked more like an office than a home. There was a drawing board in the living-room, and a word-processor.

78

'My dad works for a firm of architects,' said Peter as Holly and Miranda looked at a large page of house plans pinned to the drawing board.

He took them through into a small bedroom, as neat and tidy as the rest of the flat. On a small desk, piles of computer paper and a row of notebooks were carefully stacked.

Holly pulled out her own notebook. 'We need to write a few things down,' she said. 'We'll have to open a new file on the car, and on that man. Is it OK to sit on the bed?'

'Help yourself,' said Peter, handing the cans to the two girls.

Holly sat cross-legged on the bed. 'We need a name for the file,' she said, her pen poised over the open notebook.

'He looked like a duck the way he walked,' said Miranda. 'How about making his code-name, "the Duck"?'

'"The Duck", it is,' said Holly. She underlined the title and began to make notes about the car. Peter and Miranda sat on either side of her, reading over her shoulders as she wrote.

'Now then,' she said. 'What do we know

about the man? Apart from the way he walks.'

'I should think he works in an office,' said Peter.

'How do you make that out?' asked Miranda.

'The suit,' said Peter.

'And he doesn't have any children,' added Holly.

Miranda stared at her. 'What makes you say that?'

'He didn't know it was half-term,' said Holly with a smile. 'And I noticed he was quite vain about his appearance.'

'You're making this up as you go along,' said Miranda. 'How can you possibly work that out?'

'Didn't you see the way he combed his hair across the top of his head?' said Holly. 'So he didn't look so bald? He wouldn't do that unless he was vain. I'd say he was about forty years old,' she continued. She wrote 'big envelope' and underlined it.

'So?' said Peter. 'What have we got? A stolen car. A man who has keys to the car, but who said it wasn't *his*. And a mysterious envelope which he put in the boot.'

'And if that lot isn't dead suspicious,

I'd like to know what is,' said Holly. 'I'd love to know what was in that envelope. I'll bet it's full of secret documents.' Her imagination began to work. 'I bet he's a double agent,' she said. 'Selling top-secret information. He's probably been told to leave all the information in the boot of that car.' Her eyes lit up. 'Which must mean he left it there for someone else.'

'That's it,' said Peter. 'All we've got to do is watch the car. If you're right, someone will be coming along to pick the stuff up.' He climbed off the bed and went over to the window. 'And we can do the stake-out from here.' He looked round at the two girls, his eyes gleaming with excitement. 'No one will be able to go near the car without us spotting them.' He picked up a camera from his desk. 'We can photograph them,' he said.

'I think you're both barmy,' said Miranda. 'If you think I'm sitting here all day, staring out of the window in case someone comes along, you can think again!'

Miranda gave a heavy sigh. 'What time is it, *now*?' she asked.

Holly looked round from her perch by

the window. 'Time you got a watch,' she said.

They had been taking it in turns to sit at the window, watching the car for what seemed to Miranda to be about twenty years. No one had gone anywhere near the white car.

'I'm bored to death,' said Miranda. 'And I'm hungry.' She looked at Peter. 'Is there anything to eat?'

'I doubt it,' said Peter. 'Dad usually brings food in on his way home.'

'That does it,' said Miranda. 'I'm going to get myself something to eat before I starve.'

'I was *sure* someone would have come along by now,' said Holly.

'And what if they don't?' asked Miranda. 'What do we do? Sit here all night? And all day tomorrow, too?'

'We could go down and take some photos,' suggested Peter. 'We'll want some pictures of the car as evidence.'

Miranda jumped up, glad of any excuse to relieve the boredom. 'Can I take them?' she said, picking up the camera and putting it to her eye. She focused on Holly, who pulled a silly face.

'Do you know how to use it?' asked Peter.

82

Miranda glared at him. 'Of course!' she said. 'What do you think I am, an idiot?'

They headed down to the carpark.

'Tell you what,' Peter said to Miranda. 'You take the photos while Holly and I keep watch. We don't want anyone coming up on us unexpectedly and catching us.'

Holly and Peter went to separate corners of the block. From those locations they could keep watch on both entrances to the carpark.

Miranda took a couple of photographs of the car and then the three of them met up again at the back entrance to the block.

'Done!' Miranda said proudly. 'Now, how about something to eat? We could at least get ourselves a few packets of crisps.'

'Someone should stay here to keep watch,' said Holly. 'You know what it's like. The moment we wander off, someone will come and take the envelope without us seeing. That *always* happens on TV.'

'OK,' said Miranda. 'Give me some money. I'll do the shopping. You keep watch.' She grinned. 'And I'll bet you a million pounds that no one goes anywhere near that car.'

Holly and Peter stood in the doorway as Miranda set off for the shops.

'I'd love to know what's in that envelope,' said Holly.

'There are ways of getting into cars without the keys,' said Peter.

Holly frowned at him. '*Breaking* in, you mean?'

Peter nodded.

'Do *you* know how?' asked Holly.

'No,' admitted Peter. 'But it can't be *that* difficult.'

'I'm not breaking into the car,' Holly said firmly. 'I'm not doing anything illegal.'

Peter chewed his lip thoughtfully. 'I suppose he did remember to lock the boot?' he said. 'I mean, he was a bit flustered, wasn't he? He might have forgotten.'

Holly looked at him. 'We could go and check, couldn't we?' she said. 'Just check whether it's locked or not?'

Peter grinned. 'Come on, then,' he said.

They glanced around the deserted carpark, then made their way across towards the car.

After all, thought Holly, there was nothing so *very* bad about taking a look inside an unlocked boot. Especially if they found evidence of a crime.

*　　*　　*

Miranda came out on to the road with Peter's camera, swinging from its strap, in her hand. The shop where Peter had bought the cans of drink was on the corner, about a hundred metres away.

What a total waste of a nice day, she thought as she walked along the pavement. She hoped Holly would give up on this idea soon, or they could end up peering out of that window for the whole of their half-term holiday.

Holly's obsession with spying was beginning to test Miranda's loyalty to its limits. It was supposed to be exciting! Up to now, it had been about as exciting as watching paint dry.

A large metallic-blue car drew up to the kerb just ahead of Miranda. Two men got out. They were wearing jeans and bomber jackets. One man was stocky, with cropped blond hair and a bulldog face. The other was thin and unshaven with ratty hair that hung over his shoulders.

They ignored her as she passed them.

I don't much like the look of them, thought Miranda. She glanced round. The two men had crossed the pavement and were walking to the side of the block of flats; walking down

85

the narrow strip of pavement that led to the carpark.

The hair rose on Miranda's neck. Something about the men unsettled her. Something in the way they strode towards the carpark. As if they were in a hurry. As if they were up to something.

She paused, waiting until the two men passed out of sight around the side of the building.

You're getting as bad as Holly, thought Miranda. *They're probably just workmen or something*.

Miranda frowned. *Could* they have something to do with that car? Could Holly have been right all along? Surely not?

Miranda turned and followed their trail alongside the building. It wouldn't hurt to see where they went. And if they went anywhere near the car, she would at least be able to take a couple of quick photographs of them without being spotted.

She edged herself to the corner and looked round.

Her heart jumped into her mouth.

Over at the far corner of the carpark she could see Holly and Peter at the white car. But

86

the thing that really alarmed her was that the two men had broken into a run. They were running towards her two friends.

And they didn't seem to be the type of people to want a quiet chat.

Chased!

'It's locked,' said Peter, pulling unsuccessfully at the lid of the car's boot. He looked at Holly. 'Oh, well, it was worth a try.'

Holly shrugged, secretly quite relieved. She would have loved to have found out what was in the envelope the man had put in there, but she was not at all happy about the idea of nosing into someone else's property. It went against everything she had always been taught by her parents.

'Shall we go back and wait for Miranda?' she said.

'I suppose so,' said Peter.

'I hope something happens soon,' sighed Holly. 'I don't think Miranda is going to put up with all this sitting about for much longer. She's not the most patient person in the world. Do you think we could be completely wrong about all this? I know people are always telling me I've got an overactive imagination.'

'It wasn't your imagination that changed the number plates, was it?' said Peter. 'And it wasn't your imagination that made that man lie about the car. If only it wasn't locked . . .' He gave the lid of the boot another tug. 'I'm sure if we had the right tools, we could get in here,' he said.

'No!' Holly said firmly. 'I'm not having anything to do with that!' She turned away from the car. 'Oh!' She grabbed a fierce hold of Peter's sleeve.

Peter's head spun round. Two men were running silently towards them across the carpark. Two very unsavoury-looking men. And the expressions on their faces were enough to tell him that they meant trouble.

'Run!' yelled Peter.

Holly didn't need telling twice. These two were not like the other man: they looked much more dangerous. They looked the sort who would be much more likely to hit first and ask questions later.

Holly and Peter went skidding up the grassy slope, Holly's heart hammering away in her chest with fright.

She risked a brief glance round. The two men had passed the car and were pounding up the slope towards them.

'This way!' panted Peter, catching hold of her arm and yanking her towards the nearest of the buildings. 'We can lose them in here!'

They crashed through a pair of doors and came tumbling into a hallway. Holly had no time to catch her breath as Peter dragged her along and round a corner into a wide foyer. As they ran, Holly just had time to read a sign fixed to the wall:

Welcome to the Boxall Estate Community Centre.

The sound of their feet echoed along the corridor as they ran.

'In here!' gasped Peter, wrenching a side door open and dragging Holly in after him. They were in some sort of deserted classroom, filled with desks and with posters all over the walls.

Peter snatched the door closed and the two of them stood gulping in breath and staring at each other.

'Wait until we hear them go past,' panted

Peter. 'Then we can double back and head for my place.'

All Holly could hear was the blood pounding in her ears. There was no sound of pursuing feet beyond the door.

'Who *are* they?' gasped Holly.

'I don't know,' said Peter. 'But they weren't too pleased to see us at the car, were they?' He stared at her with round eyes. 'You were *right*, Holly. You must be!'

'Oh, crumbs,' gasped Holly. 'I wish I *wasn't*. I wish I'd never started this. I don't think I want to be a spy after all.'

Peter grinned darkly. 'It's a bit late for that,' he said.

Holly looked at him. 'Are you scared?' she asked.

'No.' He gave her a half-smile. 'Well, a *bit*.'

Holly nodded. 'Me too, a *bit*.' She spread her arms wide. 'About *this* much!'

Peter took a deep breath. 'I'm going to have a quick look. Maybe they've gone.' He cautiously opened the door a fraction. He looked out. 'No sign of them,' he said. 'Let's get out of here.'

They stepped into the hallway.

91

There was a shout from the far end. One of the men was standing there. The other came running around the corner.

'Oh, no!' gasped Holly.

They ran again. It was like a nightmare. Surely there would be someone in the Community Centre *somewhere*? All they had to do was find an adult and they'd be safe.

A curious noise hit Holly's ears. It was like a whole gang of howling cats, mixed in with something like blaring car horns and the sort of crashes and bangs refuse collectors make when they are in a bad mood.

'This way,' said Peter, jerking Holly around yet another corner. They ran up a short flight of stairs and Peter shoved his way through a door.

The noise blasted at them. Gathered in the room beyond was a whole orchestra of small children, banging away at percussion, honking into brass instruments and sawing at violins. Holly and Peter had come in behind the orchestra. At the far end of the room, a woman with wild grey hair and a long floral dress was jerking about like a scarecrow in a hurricane, her arms flapping in the air. There was a look of acute pain on her face, and her eyes were tightly closed as she hopped from foot to foot.

'With *feeling*,' she shouted above the terrible racket. 'Percussion! Keep time! Bom, bom, *bom*!'

Peter tugged at Holly's sleeve. Right at the back of the orchestra was a pair of unplayed kettledrums.

Peter put his mouth to Holly's ear.

'We can pretend to be part of the orchestra,' he said. 'In case they come in here after us.'

'We're too big,' said Holly.

Peter pulled her over to the drums and got down on his knees. He gave her an encouraging look.

She knelt down next to him, anxiously watching the door.

A few seconds later the door opened a fraction and she saw a grim pair of eyes scanning the rehearsal room.

She picked up a pair of sticks and began hammering away at the kettledrum. The face at the door winced and slid away. The door closed.

The conductor opened her eyes. 'Who on earth is making that terrible noise!' she shouted, waving the orchestra to a ragged stop. Thirty small faces turned to look at Holly and Peter.

'Sorry,' said Holly, getting to her feet. 'I've always wanted to be in an orchestra.'

Peter stood up. The woman gawped at them.

'Well, really!' she said.

'We'll go,' said Holly, edging towards the door. 'Sorry we disturbed you.' She gave a hopeful smile. 'If you ever need a drummer, just let me know,' she said as Peter yanked her out of the room.

They stood looking at each other in the corridor. There was no sign of the two men.

'Come on,' said Peter. 'Let's get out of here. We need to find Miranda!'

'Where have you been?' asked Miranda. The two friends discovered her hiding behind the doors at the back of Peter's block. 'What happened to you?'

As they headed up to Peter's flat, they filled Miranda in on their narrow escape.

'One thing's for sure,' said Holly as she peered down at the car from Peter's bedroom window. 'We're on to *something*.'

'They came back,' Miranda told them. 'The

two men. I kept out of sight. They came back to the car. And they had a key for the boot.'

'I knew it!' said Holly. 'Did they take the envelope?'

'You bet they did,' said Miranda.

'I don't suppose you thought to take any photos?' said Peter.

Miranda gave him a superior look. 'Then you suppose wrong,' she said. 'I got two or three good shots of them through the glass in the back door. And I did even better than that! The fatter one was looking at some stuff out of the envelope as he walked back. I *heard* what he said. He said, "Wednesday at ten o'clock." And the other one said, "Can we trust him?" And the fat one said, "He knows what will happen if he tries to . . ." and then they went round the corner and I couldn't hear anything else.'

'Wow!' breathed Holly. *'Wednesday at ten o'clock*? What do you think they've got planned?' Her eyes widened as a thought struck her. 'A robbery!' she said. 'That *must* be it! The Duck must have left them some inside information. You know, stuff about how to get past alarm systems and all that.' She let

95

out a long, whistling breath. 'We should go to the police.'

'No, wait,' said Peter. 'Let's think about this. My dad would go crazy if I went to the police and it all turned out to be a mistake again.'

Holly looked sharply at him. '*Again*? What do you mean, *again*?'

Peter looked sheepishly at the two girls. 'It was a couple of months ago,' he said. 'Just before we moved here. I thought a house across the road from where we lived was being burgled. There was a big van outside, see, and these men were carrying stuff out. I phoned the police.' He grinned weakly. 'They called out three police cars. But it wasn't a burglary at all. The people were moving house.'

He frowned. 'How was I supposed to know? It certainly *looked* like someone was emptying the house. I mean, you see these reports on the telly, where entire vanloads of stuff get stolen in broad daylight. I thought that was what was happening.'

'Oh, great,' said Miranda. 'So they've got you on file as an idiot, have they?'

'Actually, the police were OK about it,' said

Peter. 'But my dad hit the roof.' He looked at the two girls. 'That's why I'd rather not go to the police until we're *certain* about what's going on here. If we're wrong, my dad will ground me for the next thirty *years*.'

'So what do we do?' asked Holly. 'Wait until we read reports of the robbery in the papers, and *then* tell the police? For heaven's sake, Peter, I wish you'd mentioned this earlier.'

'Sorry,' said Peter. 'I didn't think.'

'Then we'd better *start* thinking,' said Holly. 'It's a pity we didn't get a photo of the Duck at the car. That would have tied everything up nicely.'

'He might come back,' Peter said hopefully. 'If we keep the car under really close surveillance we might get the chance to photograph him. That way, if there *is* a robbery, at least we'll be able to give all our information to the police to help them track the robbers down. After all,' he continued, 'we don't have the faintest clue *where* the robbery is going to happen, even if we're right about it.'

'I suppose that makes sense,' said Holly.

'Do you mean we've got to sit here for the next two days on the off-chance that the Duck comes back?' said Miranda.

'No,' said Peter. 'You don't have to do that. I'll keep watch. And I'll phone you the moment I see anything.'

'Well, good luck!' said Miranda. 'If you ask me, you'll be wasting your time. Why should he come back? If we're right, he's already passed all the information on to the robbers. If they *are* robbers.'

'Let's see what's in the photographs before we decide anything,' said Peter.

'OK,' said Holly. 'We'll give it that long, and then we'll meet up again and decide what to do. What do you say, Miranda? We'll come over here tomorrow afternoon and talk about it.'

Miranda shrugged. 'If you say so,' she said. 'But if we're going to be stuck in here for hours staring at that stupid car, Peter, you might at least get some biscuits or something in. I'm half-starved.'

'Oh, crumbs!' exclaimed Holly at Miranda's mention of food. 'I've still got all that shopping to do!'

'Could you drop the film off at a chemist's

on your way?' asked Peter. 'I'll stay here to keep watch.'

The two girls waited while he unloaded the film from his camera.

'We'll pick up the film on the way round here tomorrow,' Holly told him as they left. She grinned. 'And then we'll see how good Miranda is at photographing criminals.'

'*Possible* criminals,' said Miranda, giving Peter a doubtful look. 'After what you've just told us, I'm not at all sure about any of this. It wouldn't surprise me in the least if it turned out that the Duck had *sold* the car to those two, and the envelope just had the car's documents in it.'

'What about the altered number plates?' said Holly.

'We've only got Peter's word for that,' said Miranda. 'And two shiny screws. All the rest is just in your *mind*.'

'No,' Holly said determinedly. 'It's not just my imagination this time. I'm certain there's something going on.'

Miranda sighed. 'Aren't you always?' She laughed. 'Oh, come on, let's get that shopping done. We'll find out if the pair of you are right when we watch the news

99

on Wednesday. But I'll bet you anything you like there'll be some perfectly innocent explanation for all of this.'

Holly shook her head. No matter what Miranda might think, she *knew* they were really on to something. A real crime for Spies-R-Us to solve!

 'The Duck'

It was the following afternoon. Holly had phoned Peter a couple of times during the day to check whether he had seen anyone at the car. He had sounded quite fed up. There was nothing to report. No one had gone anywhere near the car and, he told her forlornly, he'd been sitting staring out of his bedroom window all morning.

Holly met up with Miranda and they picked up the developed photographs.

'Let me see, let me see,' Miranda insisted as they came out of the chemist's with the envelope of photographs.

'No,' Holly insisted. 'We'll wait until we get to Peter's place. Then we'll *all* look at them.'

They were in for a shock when they gathered in Peter's bedroom and took out the photographs. The first few were fine. Pictures of various cars and scenes that

101

Peter had obviously taken some time previously.

There were only seven photographs. For some reason the shop hadn't printed any of the ones Miranda had taken.

'That's odd,' said Peter. 'Where are the others?'

'Typical!' said Miranda. 'You can't trust anyone these days! What are they playing at?'

'Just a minute,' said Peter. 'Let's take a look at the negatives.' He drew out the thin strip of negatives and held them to the light from the window. 'They're all blank,' he said. 'There's nothing there.'

'Don't be daft,' said Miranda. 'There must be.'

'Look for yourself,' said Peter, handing her the strips of film. He gave Miranda a sudden suspicious look. 'You *did* remember to take the lens cap off, didn't you?'

'What lens cap?' said Miranda.

Peter gave a groan.

'Now look here,' said Miranda. 'No one told me anything about any lens caps.'

'Oh, Miranda!' moaned Holly. 'You twit!'

'Well,' sighed Peter. 'That's our best bit of evidence down the drain.'

'It's not my fault,' said Miranda.

'Then whose fault is it?' asked Peter.

'Yours, for not telling me about the lens cap,' said Miranda.

'Let's not argue about it,' said Holly. 'Let's decide what we do next. We still know what the men look like, so it's not a total disaster. We'll just have to rely on our memories.' She took out her notebook. 'So,' she said. 'First of all we write down a detailed description of those two men. At least if the robbery happens we'll be able to give the police a good description of the suspects.'

'Hmm,' said Miranda. '*If* it happens.'

It wasn't a very entertaining afternoon. Holly's visions of taking a whole batch of incriminating photographs to the police had evaporated. She tried not to blame Miranda for the disaster, but it was a let-down, and it was difficult to make friendly conversation under the circumstances.

'I suppose the best we can do is carry on watching the car,' said Peter, 'now that we don't have any photos.'

But Miranda wasn't in the mood for another long vigil at the window. She could tell Holly was annoyed at her, and it made her bad-tempered and snappy.

After about half an hour of awkwardly silent car-watching, Miranda got up. 'I'm going home,' she said. 'I'm sick and tired of this. Perhaps the two of *you* ought to be Spies-R-Us. You don't seem to need me!'

'Miranda!' said Holly. 'Don't be like that.'

'I'm not being like anything,' said Miranda. 'I'm going home.' She gave Holly a hard look. 'I hope the two of you have a really *interesting* time!'

Holly looked unhappily at Peter as they heard the front door slam.

'I'd better go after her,' said Holly.

'OK,' said Peter. 'Tell her I'm sorry I was nasty about the photos. It wasn't really her fault. I'll ring you if anything happens.'

Holly caught up with Miranda on the stairs.

'I don't want us to fall out,' she said. 'Come on, Miranda; we're best friends, aren't we?'

Miranda's scowl softened. 'Yes,' she said. 'Of course we are. I just feel so stupid about those photos. And I really don't want to spend any more time watching that car.'

'We don't have to,' said Holly with a smile.

'Peter can do that for us.' She laughed. 'That's what boys are for,' she said. 'Doing all the *boring* stuff. Look, Mum said that if I met her at the bank at closing-time, she'd take me shopping for some new clothes. Do you fancy coming with me? You can help me choose. You know you're better at choosing nice stuff than I am. How about it?'

'OK,' said Miranda, her usual good nature rapidly returning. 'And next time, if there is a next time, I'll remember to take the lens cap off the camera before I try taking any pictures.'

The two reconciled friends linked arms and set off for the bank where Mrs Adams worked.

'Tell me honestly,' said Holly as they walked along the road. 'Do you think I've let my imagination run away with me about this robbery?'

'I don't know,' said Miranda. 'It wouldn't be exactly unheard of, would it?'

'But Peter seems pretty sure, too,' said Holly.

'Yes,' Miranda said drily. 'And let's not forget that he started all this. And let's not forget that earlier business with the non-burglary he told us about.'

'I know,' said Holly. 'That's what makes me wonder. If he was wrong about the number plates being different then the whole thing really could be totally innocent, couldn't it? Even being chased by those two men. I mean, if my dad saw a couple of kids lurking about near his car, he'd probably chase them off. Oh, look! There's Mum!'

They were on the far side of the road from the bank where Mrs Adams worked. There was a lot of traffic between them, and as a bus passed Holly saw several people come out of the bank with her mother. One man turned to shut the doors while the others walked off. Mrs Adams stood on the pavement, as if waiting to speak to him.

'Holly!' gasped Miranda. 'Holly, for heaven's sake, look! Look at *him*!'

Even as Holly struggled for a clear view of the man between the passing traffic, the man turned, said something to her mother and walked rapidly away.

The man was in a navy-blue suit. Holly didn't catch sight of his face, but even from behind she could see the way the man's

106

thinning hair was combed over his scalp. But the thing that really made Holly's mouth drop open in amazement was the way the man walked. Splay-footedly. Almost *waddling*!

'It's the *Duck*,' gasped Miranda. She stared at Holly. 'The Duck works at your mum's bank!'

The two girls goggled at each other.

'*Wednesday at ten o'clock*,' said Miranda. 'That's what those two men were saying. You don't think he's helped them set up a robbery of the bank, do you?'

'No,' said Holly. 'No, it can't be that. I remember my mum saying that all the money is taken off in a security van on a Tuesday. That was today. There'll hardly be any money in there at all tomorrow.'

'But would *they* know that?' said Miranda.

'Of course they would,' said Holly. 'If he was helping them with a robbery, he'd have told them, wouldn't he?' Holly couldn't believe that someone who worked alongside her mother could be involved in anything criminal. 'It must be something else.'

'Such as what?' asked Miranda.

'Who knows?' said Holly. 'Maybe you were right, and he's sold the car to those men.

Something simple like that. Look, let's go over there, but don't say *anything* about any of this to my mum. Let's just find out exactly who he is first.'

They crossed the road.

'Hello, you two,' said Mrs Adams. 'Ready for the shops?'

Holly nodded. 'We saw you from across the road,' she said cautiously. 'Who was the man who locked up the bank?'

'The one with the waddle,' added Miranda.

Mrs Adams put her hand over her mouth to hide a smile. 'That's not a very kind thing to say,' she said. 'Even if it's true.'

'But who is he?' asked Holly. 'I think I've seen him around before.'

'That,' said Mrs Adams, 'is my new boss, Norman Cheevers. The new manager. Come on, you two, let's go and get the car.'

Holly and Miranda glanced at one another behind Mrs Adams's back.

'The *manager*?' mouthed Miranda.

Holly gave a puzzled shrug. 'We'll talk about it later,' she whispered. 'With Peter.'

'What are you girls whispering about?' asked Mrs Adams.

'Oh, nothing,' said Holly. 'Nothing at all.'

One thing was quite clear in Holly's mind. Whatever Mr Cheevers was up to with that curious car parked at the back of Peter's block of flats, it certainly couldn't be a plan to rob his own bank!

A shocking discovery

It was later that evening. Miranda had arranged with her mother to stay the night at Holly's house. The two girls were in Holly's bedroom, munching their way through a supper of burgers and chips.

Holly looked gloomily at the shoe-box on her bed. Inside were a pair of sensible school shoes. 'I wouldn't have bothered turning up to meet my mum if I'd known *these* were all I was getting,' she said, giving the box a shove with her elbow. 'Boring shoes!'

'That's probably why your mum didn't let on,' Miranda said through a mouthful of chips. 'Mums can be dead sneaky like that.'

'Tell me about it!' sighed Holly. 'School shoes! The most boring items of clothing in the entire world.'

'Still,' Miranda said cheerfully. 'If we *hadn't*

110

met your mum, we wouldn't have seen the Duck, would we?'

'No,' admitted Holly. She took a large bite of burger and chewed thoughtfully. 'But what on earth do you think he's up to?' Holly stared down at her page of notes.

'Go through it again while I have a think,' said Miranda.

'OK,' said Holly. 'We've got a suspicious car.'

'Check,' said Miranda, lying on her back on Holly's bed and dropping chips one by one into her mouth. 'Suspicious car. Possibly stolen.'

'The Duck turns up. He says it isn't his, but he has keys to the boot,' continued Holly. 'He leaves an envelope in the boot.' She ticked the entries in her notebook as she went along. 'Two nasty-looking types chase Peter and me away and take the envelope. One of them mentions something about ten o'clock Wednesday.'

'Which is tomorrow,' said Miranda. 'Unless they mean *next* Wednesday.' She chewed. 'Or the Wednesday after.'

'The Duck is the bank manager,' read Holly. 'But all this can't possibly be anything

111

to do with a bank raid, because we know from my mum that all the money is taken away on a Tuesday.' She looked up at Miranda, who was leaning over the side of the bed in search of a lost chip. 'Any bright ideas?'

'I was thinking about something you said last week,' said Miranda, picking the lost chip up off the floor and wiping it on her sleeve. 'You know? When we were first following Peter?' She studied the chip for a moment then popped it into her mouth. 'About kidnapping? What if the Duck has arranged with those two men to have himself kidnapped? *Pretend* kidnapped, I mean. Held to ransom for a huge amount of money.'

'That's not bad,' Holly said admiringly. 'No one would suspect he'd have anything to do with his own kidnapping.'

'No one except Spies-R-Us,' said Miranda.

Holly got up off the carpet. 'I'm going to phone Peter,' she said. 'We ought to let him know what we've found out.'

She ran downstairs, coming to a puzzled halt just inside the living-room. The telephone was missing. 'Mum?' she called. 'Where's the phone?'

'Come and see,' called Mrs Adams from the

kitchen. Holly went through. Her mother had the telephone on the kitchen table. In bits.

'You can thank your brother for this,' said Mrs Adams. 'I've told him not to play ball-games in the living-room.'

'Is it broken?' asked Holly.

'It's not *working*, if that's what you mean,' said her mother. She poked at the innards of the telephone with a screwdriver. 'I don't know what he's done to it.' She sighed and pushed the bits away. 'I'll have to phone for a repair man when I get to work tomorrow,' she said. 'As if I don't have enough to do.' She looked at Holly. 'Your brother is a menace.'

Holly went back up to Miranda and told her about Jamie's accident with the telephone.

'I've been thinking some more,' said Miranda. 'I bet they're going to use *that* car in the kidnapping.'

'If that's true,' said Holly, 'those two men will be over at Peter's place some time before ten tomorrow morning to pick the car up. Do you think I should tell Mum about all of this?'

'What if we're wrong?' said Miranda.

Holly nodded. 'That's what I was thinking,' she said. 'We'd look complete fools if we

113

told everyone, and then nothing happened.' She frowned. 'I don't know what to do.'

'I'll tell you what,' said Miranda. 'Let's go over to Peter's place first thing tomorrow. We can tell him all about the Duck, and we can make sure we get some good photos of the men if they turn up to take the car.'

'*When* they turn up,' said Holly.

Miranda looked at her. 'I prefer *if* at the moment,' she said. 'After all, it's only a *theory*.'

'It's a very *good* theory,' said Holly. 'Imagine the look on everyone's faces when we show them photos of the kidnappers and tell them how the whole thing was set up with the Duck himself!' She grinned. 'Are we brilliant detectives, or what? We'll probably get our names in the papers. Or on TV, even. Wow!'

Miranda laughed. 'Slow down, Holly. Nothing's actually happened yet.'

'Oh, but it *will*,' said Holly. 'I *hope*.'

The two friends spent the rest of the evening giving each other mock interviews for news bulletins.

'Holly Adams,' said Miranda, pretending

to be holding a microphone under Holly's nose. 'When did you first suspect there was a kidnapping planned?'

'Oh, it was when I noticed that the number plates had been switched on the car,' said Holly.

'You fibber!' exclaimed Miranda. 'That was Peter!'

'Well, yes,' admitted Holly. 'But we did most of the actual detective work, didn't we?'

'How should I know?' said Miranda. 'I'm being a TV reporter.'

'Then how did you know about Peter?'

The interview dissolved into laughter.

They didn't get to sleep until quite late, and Holly's parents had already gone off to work by the time the two friends were up and about the following morning.

They went down to fix themselves a quick breakfast before going over to Peter's flat. Jamie had transformed the kitchen table into a battleground for a game of alien invaders.

'You shouldn't be playing in here,' said Holly.

Jamie glared sulkily at her. 'Everyone's on at me today,' he said. 'Mum's grounded me

115

for two days because I accidentally bashed the rotten telephone with my ball.'

'You shouldn't have been playing in there either,' Holly said heartlessly. 'It serves you right.'

'She said I was a menace,' said Jamie. 'Me! I could understand it if she'd been talking about you! And she's only in a rotten mood because of stuff at work. She was telling Dad about it.'

'If that's true, then you should at least be bright enough to keep out of trouble,' said Holly. 'You know what Mum's like.'

There was a ring at the door.

Holly went to answer it. It was Peter.

'I've been trying to ring you,' he said as she let him in. 'I think there's something wrong with your phone.'

Holly told him about Jamie and the phone as she led him into the kitchen.

'Hey!' said Miranda. 'Shouldn't you be watching the car?'

'I'm going straight back,' said Peter. 'I thought you might like to come with me. It's dead boring watching it all on my own.'

Jamie's ears pricked up. 'Why are you watching a car?' he asked.

116

'It's none of your business,' said Holly.

Jamie poked his tongue out at her.

'Tell Peter about the Duck,' said Miranda. 'Tell him what we've worked out.'

Holly explained about Norman Cheevers being her mother's boss at the bank.

'Wow!' said Peter with a low whistle. 'A bank robbery!'

'No,' said Holly. 'We've already ruled that out. The security van takes all the money away on Tuesday.' She looked proudly at Miranda. 'We think it's going to be—'

'Waaah!' yelled Jamie, his eyes like saucers. 'Holly!'

'Shut up, Jamie,' snapped Holly. 'You shouldn't even be listening. This is private.'

'But, *listen*!' howled Jamie. 'They *didn't*! Mum was saying this morning!'

The three friends stared at him.

'What are you talking about, Jamie?' asked Holly.

'At breakfast,' Jamie said breathlessly. 'Mum was talking to Dad about it at breakfast. She was really annoyed 'cos her boss had *changed* things. And she said – I heard her, Holly, I *heard* her! She said the security van was coming *this morning*!'

'*What*?' yelled Holly.

'Jamie,' gasped Miranda. 'Are you sure about this?'

'Of course I am!' howled Jamie.

Peter stared at his watch. 'It's half past nine,' he said. 'That means they could be doing the robbery in *half an hour*! Quick! We've got to phone the police!'

'We can't phone from here,' said Holly. 'The phone's broken.' She stared at her friends. 'There's time to get to the bank,' she said. 'We can warn my mum. She'll know what to do.'

They ran helter-skelter into the hall.

'I'm coming, too!' shouted Jamie.

'No!' said Holly. 'You go next door. Tell Mrs Griebler to phone the police. Say she's to tell them there's going to be a robbery at Mum's bank.'

'But—'

'*Do* it, Jamie!' shouted Holly. 'And tell her we've gone to warn Mum.'

'She won't *believe* me!' yelled Jamie.

'Yes, she will,' said Holly, snatching the front door open. 'Just *go*, Jamie! Please! This isn't a *joke*!'

They ran frantically along the road. Holly's heart was battering at her ribs. *I should have said something to Mum*, she was thinking in desperation. *I should have told her. What are we going to do if we're too late? It'll be all our fault! What if someone gets hurt?*

These terrible thoughts spurred her on as they raced towards the street, only a few roads away, where Holly's mother worked.

They ran along the pavement, Holly in the lead, dodging between pedestrians.

She heard a howl from behind her. She glanced round. Peter had crashed into someone and was sprawled on the pavement. Miranda stopped to help him. But Holly didn't have time to worry about that. She had to get to the bank!

She came pelting around the final corner. The big white security van was parked at the kerb, but there was no sign of any security guards. They had arrived early. And they must already be inside.

Holly rushed up the steps and sent the doors crashing open. She came to a skidding halt, her eyes wide with fear, her heart leaping into her mouth.

She was too late. The robbery was already taking place!

The Mystery Kids

Holly stifled a scream. Half a dozen people were lying face down on the floor – including two security guards with padded jackets and white helmets. Only two men were on their feet: both were wearing masks and one of them was holding a gun. As the door crashed shut behind Holly, the gunman turned towards her.

Holly recognised the men despite their masks. They were the two men who had chased her and Peter away from the car.

The man with the gun had a large white case at his feet. The other carried a hold-all. A terrified-looking bank clerk was pushing bundles of notes over the counter, and the other man was stuffing them into the bag. Behind the glass screens, Holly saw several more frightened faces.

121

'Get *down*!' shouted the man with the gun. 'On your face! Now!'

Holly didn't need telling twice. She threw herself to the floor, trembling all over. She was too late to do anything. Too late to do anything other than lie shaking with terror with the other innocent bystanders.

'Let's go!' shouted the gunman.

Holly didn't even dare look up as she heard heavy feet pound past her head.

'Anyone who moves in the next five minutes *gets* it!'

She heard the sound of the doors swinging closed. There were a few seconds of terrible silence.

'The alarm!' someone shouted. 'Hit the alarm!'

Holly lifted her head. The other customers and the two guards were getting to their feet, with stunned looks on their faces.

Holly got to her knees. Her legs felt like jelly.

'Is anyone hurt?' Beyond the glass screen she saw Mr Cheevers staring out with a very convincing look of shock on his face.

One of the guards helped a woman to her feet. A babble of voices filled the bank as people began to recover from their brief ordeal. There were more people behind the screens now, as bank workers came running from other rooms to see what had happened.

'Keep calm, everyone,' shouted one of the guards above the rising noise. 'It's all over. There's no danger now. Keep calm, please, the police will be here in a few minutes.'

Holly stumbled to her feet, leaning against the wall. The shock made her feel giddy.

'Holly!' It was her mother's voice. Holly stared through the glass at her mother's horrified face.

'Mum!'

Mrs Adams ran to the side door and wrenched it open. Two seconds later they were hugging each other tightly.

'Holly! Are you all right?' gasped her mother.

'Yes,' panted Holly, her head swimming.

'What are you *doing* here?' groaned Mrs Adams.

Holly pointed a shaking finger towards Mr Cheevers.

'It was *him*!' she shouted. 'He's in league with the robbers! I was trying to warn you, but I was too late!'

'What?' Mrs Adams stared at her. 'Holly? What are you talking about?'

Holly took a deep breath. 'We *saw* him!' she shouted. 'At the car. He pretended it wasn't his, but he had the keys. He left an envelope in the boot.' She stared up at her mother. 'Then *those* two men came and took the envelope! We saw everything!'

Mrs Adams's face looked confused and disbelieving.

'Holly? What car? What envelope? What *is* all this?'

Mr Cheevers was standing at the open side door, his mouth fallen open as he looked at Holly.

'Ask Miranda if you don't believe me!' yelled Holly. 'He helped plan the robbery!'

Everyone was looking at her now.

'Poor thing,' said someone. 'It's the shock.'

Holly was almost bursting with exasperation. Not one of the dozen or so faces that surrounded her showed any sign of believing her.

124

Mr Cheevers shut his mouth. Holly saw his Adam's apple bobbing as he swallowed.

'I think we'd better get the child a chair,' he said. 'She's had a nasty shock.'

'I don't need a chair,' said Holly. She looked at her mother. 'Why doesn't anyone *believe* me? Why else would I be here if I wasn't telling the truth? Mum? Please! You've *got* to believe me!'

Mrs Adams looked into Holly's face.

At that moment the doors burst open and two police officers came running in.

'Has anyone been hurt?' asked one of them.

'No,' shouted Mr Cheevers. 'Everyone is quite safe. But they've taken all the money! The entire week's money!'

'Please!' cried Holly, breaking away from her mother and facing the police officers. 'Listen to me, please!' She flung an arm towards Mr Cheevers. 'He was in on it!'

'Now, then,' barked Mr Cheevers. 'I've had enough of this! What is this child talking about?'

The bank doors opened again and Holly saw Miranda and Peter, their faces pale, standing in the doorway.

'We were too late,' Holly shouted at them.

'It's OK,' said Miranda. 'We saw the car they drove off in. It was the same one I saw them with yesterday. Not the white one. The *blue* one.'

One of the officers spun round. 'What's going on here? You kids shouldn't be in here. Don't you know there's been a robbery?'

'Of course we *know*!' said Holly. 'We know everything!' And you're letting them get away!'

'Another police car went after them,' said Peter. He looked at the police officers. 'I can tell you where they'll switch cars!'

'You shouldn't be standing here listening to this nonsense!' howled Mr Cheevers. 'You should be hunting those men down!'

'Oh, shut up!' yelled Miranda. 'We know all about *you*! And we've got photographs to prove it!' She looked at the astonished police officers. 'We've got photos of him *and* the robbers.' She stared at Mr Cheevers. 'You didn't know we'd taken photos, did you? They're at Peter's house. Photos of you, and the robbers *and* the car! Let's see you talk your way out of *that*!'

Mr Cheevers's face went very pale and he

fell against the doorway as if his legs had given way under him.

'They'll switch to a white Cortina that's parked in the Boxall Road Estate,' said Peter. 'Quick! For heaven's sake! Tell someone!'

The police officers stared at each other.

'Get on to the station,' said one of them. 'A white Cortina. Boxall Road Estate.'

'At *last*!' gasped Holly. She looked at her mother. '*Now* will you listen to me?'

Peter grinned. 'They won't get far in the Cortina,' he said. 'I let the tyres down.'

One of the police officers began talking rapidly into his shoulder radio transmitter. The other caught hold of Miranda and Peter and pulled them in front of him.

'Now,' he said. 'Tell me what all this is about.'

'You bet we will!' said Holly.

Over by the side door, Mr Cheevers gave a low groan and sank to the floor, his face a sickly green colour.

'There's no need for that,' he moaned, as everyone else in the bank stared at him. 'I'll tell you everything.'

'Well, well,' said Mr Adams, spreading the

newspaper out on the kitchen table. 'Who'd have believed it, eh?'

Mrs Adams was there as well, and Jamie and Peter and Miranda. All gathered in the Adams kitchen the following evening.

There were two whole columns about the burglary. The headline was *MYSTERY KIDS FOIL BANK ROBBERY*. There was a photo of Mr Cheevers, and another photo of Holly, Miranda and Peter standing beside the white car, grinning sheepishly into the camera.

'Why isn't there a photo of me?' complained Jamie, pushing in under Holly's arm. 'I got Mrs Griebler to call the police.'

'Stop moaning,' said Holly.

'But I'm not even mentioned!' said Jamie.

'Here you are,' said Holly, pulling out a pen from the drawer. At the bottom of the article she wrote *PS – Jamie helped as well*. 'Will that do you?' she asked.

'No, not really,' said Jamie.

'Read that bit about the photos again,' said Miranda. 'That's my favourite bit.'

'OK,' said Mr Adams. 'Here we go. "Police say that Norman Cheevers was tricked into giving a full confession when Miranda Hunt convinced him that the youngsters had taken

128

several photographs of him and the thieves. It was only later that the girl admitted that the photographs had not come out." '

'Yesss!' crowed Miranda with a yell of laughter. 'We got him with that one! Imagine his face when he found out there weren't any photos at all! Talk about sick!'

'And what about this bit?' said Holly. '"The trio of young detectives had been keeping watch on the intended getaway car for several days, after becoming suspicious when they noticed that the number plates had been altered."' She grinned. '*Young detectives*, eh? That's us!'

'And there's even stuff about us wanting to be spy-catchers and everything,' beamed Miranda. 'I like *this* bit: "It was their fascination with mysteries that first made the young crime-busters suspect that there was something of a criminal nature going on." Whoo!'

'I hope they put him away for years and years,' said Holly.

'I expect they will,' said Mrs Adams. 'Judges always come down hard on people who abuse positions of trust.'

The article also mentioned how the police

129

had cornered the two robbers in the carpark behind Peter's flats, and how the villains had been so amazed to find the tyres had been let down that the police had managed to grab them without a shot being fired.

'I hope you don't make a habit of letting people's tyres down,' said Mr Adams.

'Hardly!' Peter said with an anxious look.

'He's only kidding you,' said Holly. 'I think we should celebrate this, you know.'

'Quite right,' said Mr Adams. He drew some money out of his wallet. 'Why don't the three of you go and treat yourselves to a burger. On me. I think you deserve it.'

'And that's not the only thing to celebrate,' said Mrs Adams. 'The area manager turned up at the bank this morning.' She smiled round at them. 'They've decided to promote the assistant manager up to full manager as of today.' Her smile widened. 'And yours truly is at the top of the list to take over as assistant manager!'

Half an hour later, the three friends were sitting in Allan's Burger Bar, chatting about their triumph.

'It looks like Spies-R-Us have got a new

partner,' said Holly, smiling at Peter. 'If you're interested?'

'You bet,' said Peter. 'If Miranda doesn't object, that is.'

Miranda looked up, her cheeks sunken from sucking at her strawberry milkshake. 'No objections here,' she said. 'If it wasn't for your weird obsession with car number plates, we'd still be wandering around making notes about innocent old ladies.'

'Or innocent boys,' said Peter. 'There is one thing, though, if you don't mind me mentioning it?'

'What's that?' asked Holly.

'Spies-R-Us is a rotten name,' said Peter.

Holly gave him an injured look. 'Oh, yes?' she said. 'I suppose you can come up with something better, can you?'

Peter smiled, flicking his hair out of his eyes. 'I think so,' he said. 'It was the headline in the newspaper that gave me the idea.'

'Which is . . . ?' asked Miranda.

'The Mystery Kids!' said Peter.

Holly picked a chip out of her box and held it in the air. 'The Mystery Kids!' she said. Peter and Miranda each held a chip.

'One for all, and all for one!' said Miranda

as they crossed the three chips in the air between them.

Holly glanced out of the window and her eyes suddenly became circular.

'Look!' she said. 'There's a woman over there taking car numbers! I wonder what she's up to?'

Her two friends followed the line of her eyes.

'For heaven's sake, Holly!' said Miranda. 'That's a traffic warden!'

'That's what she *wants* us to believe,' said Holly. 'If you want to know what I think—'

'We don't!' interrupted Miranda. 'Shut up and eat your burger, Holly! Haven't you had enough excitement to be getting on with?'

'No,' said Holly, her eyes bright with a new challenge. 'Nowhere *near* enough!'

If you enjoyed reading SPY-CATCHERS! you might also like the second title in The Mystery Kids series, also published by Hodder Children's Books

LOST AND FOUND

by Fiona Kelly

Holly is desperate for a mystery to solve – and when she sees a suspicious-looking man throw his wallet from the bus, she *knows* she's found one!

Her friends, Miranda and Peter, aren't so sure. When they go back to find the wallet, it's empty. Empty except some sort of ticket – and there's nothing mysterious about that.

Or is there . . .?

When Holly Adams is fifteen years old, she and her family move out of London. At her new school, Holly sets up The Mystery Club with Tracy Foster and Belinda Hayes.

Join The Mystery Club in its first adventure

SECRET CLUES

by Fiona Kelly

Holly could hear the blood pounding in her ears. She looked cautiously round the corner into the hall. It was deserted. 'Come on,' she whispered. 'It's our only chance.'

Suddenly there came an ominous sound: a key turning in a lock. Holly ran for the doors, but she was too late. The caretaker had locked them in with two dangerous men . . .

The three friends stumble on the clues to a lost fortune and suddenly The Mystery Club is involved in an adventure that's only too real. Before they know it, they're on a roller-coaster of mystery, danger and suspense!

THE MYSTERY KIDS SERIES
Fiona Kelly

☐ 61989 9 **SPY-CATCHERS!** £2.99

☐ 61990 2 **LOST AND FOUND** £2.99

☐ 61991 0 **TREASURE HUNT** £2.99
(July 1995)

☐ 61992 9 **THE EMPTY HOUSE** £2.99
(July 1995)

☐ 61993 7 **SMUGGLERS BAY** £2.99
(Sept. 1995)

☐ 61994 5 **FUNNY MONEY** £2.99
(Sept. 1995)

All Hodder Children's books are available at your local bookshop or newsagent, or can be ordered direct from the publisher. Just tick the titles you want and fill in the form below. Prices and availability subject to change without notice.

Hodder Children's Books, Cash Sales Department, Bookpoint, 39 Milton Park, Abingdon, OXON, OX14 4TD, UK. If you have a credit card you may order by telephone – 01235 831700.

Please enclose a cheque or postal order made payable to Bookpoint Ltd to the value of the cover price and allow the following for postage and packing:
UK & BFPO: £1.00 for the first book, 50p for the second book and 30p for each additional book ordered up to a maximum charge of £3.00.
OVERSEAS & EIRE: £2.00 for the first book, £1.00 for the second book and 50p for each additional book.

Name ....

Address ....

....

....

If you would prefer to pay by credit card, please complete:
Please debit my Visa / Access / Diner's Card / American Express (delete as applicable) card no:

Signature ....

Expiry Date ....